Merlin's Return

Robin W. Wells

Preface

Merlin was a myth. Well, that is what everybody believes, until now. The story of Merlin was nothing more than that, a story, embellished over many decades, especially with the fictitious Arthurian connection. These stories were started way back in 1136 when Geoffrey of Monmouth wrote Historia Regum Britanniae. He may have based Merlin on an amalgamation of previous historical and legendary figures, which may or may not have lived.

On top of that, Geoffrey had written three different versions of the stories, spaced out over a number of years, all variations on the same theme, all with subtle differences, making them seem individual. So, when Martin Ambrose found out he was related to a myth, he didn't know what to think. What does anybody do with that sort of knowledge? He certainly couldn't achieve any magical performances himself, nor did he particularly want to. That was until one day, he did one act unknowingly. The consequences could have been devastating, and not necessarily for the right reasons.

What unfolded was far from magical, especially when murder, theft, and deceit are all involved just to obtain some very old parchments. And the only person who could retrieve them was Martin himself.

Acknowledgements

My Granddaughter, Imogen Jones, as a nurse has given me guidance with regards to things medical. But most of all, has encouraged and pushed me to have this, my second book published.

I would also like to thank the British Museum for their incredible assistance and contribution into related material, offering both an on-line service, as well as being able to approach their staff for guidance and support.

Author's Note

The area described in this book is an especially beautiful part of Wales.

The Llangollen Railway runs through this valley to Corwen, mostly along the riverside. Further downstream, the famous Pontcysyllte Aqueduct, built by Thomas Telford in 1805, crosses the Dee Valley.

Both the Grouse Inn and the Berwyn Arms are excellent eating houses, serving locals and tourists alike.

The places mentioned in the book are all factual. There are large rock formations at the base of the Berwyn Mountain range, but any resemblance to Merlin and the cave is entirely fictitious—as are all the people, their names, and the farms described.

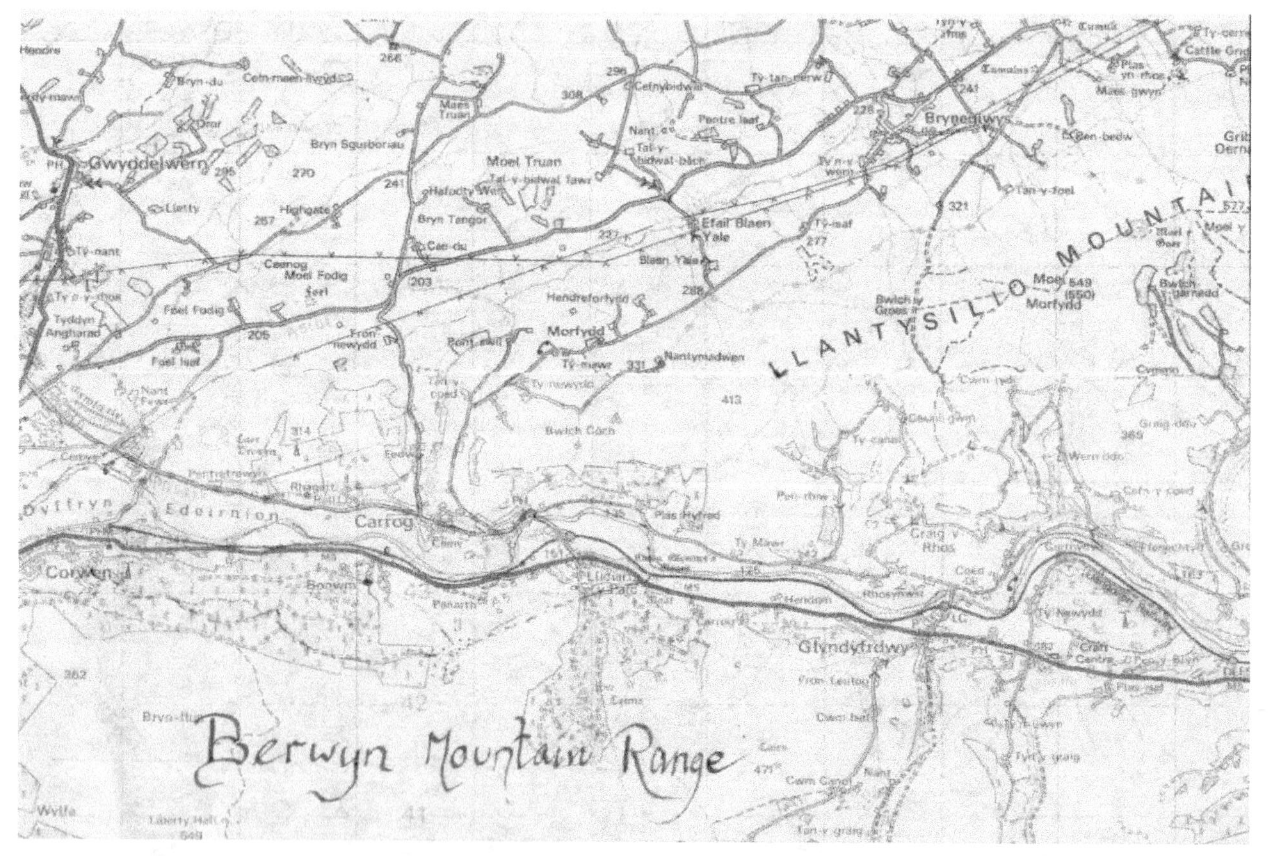

Berwyn Mountain Range
LLANTYSILIO MOUNTAIN
Gwyddelwern
Bryneglwys
Moel Truan
Efail Blaen Yale
Blaen Yale
Morfydd
Hendreforfydd
Nantymudwen
Carrog
Corwen
Glyndyfrdwy
Dyffryn Edeirnion
Moel Fodig
Foel Fodig
Foel Isaf
Bryn Sgurboriau
Bryn Tangor
Cae-du
Highgate
Lletty
Ty-nant
Bryn-du
Cefn-maen-llwyd
Maes Truan
Cefnybidwal
Tal-y-bidwal-bâch
Tal-y-bidwal fawr
Hafodty Wen
Pentre Isaf
Ty-tan-derw
Ty-'n-y wern
Tan-y-foel
Moel 549 (550) Morfydd
Bwlch y Groes
Bwlch Garnedd
Bwlch Coch
Ty-mawr
Ty-newydd
Ty-'n-y coed
Pont-faen
Pentrefelin
Rhagatt
Plas Hyfryd
Ty Mawr
Craig y Rhos
Per-rhiw
Ty canol
Cwm rhôs
Cwm isaf
Llidiart y Parc
Bonwm
Penarth
Pen-llan
Hendom
Rhosymwl
LG
Fron-Leutog
Lens
Craft Centre
Ty Newydd
Fron-Leuton
Wylfa
Liberty Hall
Bryn-llus
Cymau
Cwm Canol
Tir-y-graig
Glan-y-llyn
Wern ddu
203
205
241
257
270
296
266
308
296
228
241
321
277
288
331
413
314
125
181
382
42
41

Chapter One

Martin Ambrose had shaved every morning, looking in the same mirror on the same bathroom cabinet in the same house, for the last twenty-five years, and that same face had peered back at him for the same amount of time, then going to the same place of work for even a longer period. His face had more lines than he remembered, and his hair had started to develop steel grey strands at the sides. So, what had happened in all those years he was thinking about? On reflection, they had just flashed by, and ironically, he could barely remember any of it. There were times on his holidays that were memorable. There was also the time when he was elated when they made him a partner in the firm. He even got engaged twenty years ago. Was it really as long ago as that? But really, very little had happened in all that time.

It was that particular morning, and for no particular reason, that morning he had decided a change was needed, and since Martin had been approaching 50, he had been thinking of doing something different anyway. A thought came to him: Is this what people had called a life-changing move? And does that life-changing move include retirement? Something which he had been thinking of many times of late. But if he did retire, what would he do? He did little now other than go to work and look in the mirror as he aged. Even to the extent of committing those thoughts and many others to a list, which had included fast cars, sky-diving, and cold-water wild swimming, but none had taken his fancy. Martin was an architect by profession. He had spent a lifetime with properties, both with the design and the organisation of labour to fulfil that particular project. He had designed and built for many different types of properties and for many different clients, both commercially and privately.

Over the years, he had built up a good portfolio, which included several properties he had converted into comfortable accommodation, which he let out, and the nice house he had designed and built for himself as his main residence, where he now lived. Lastly, he also owned a property in North Wales, which he had bought on a whim. This property was on a time when coming home from a visit to Snowdonia. Was it this that had turned out to be the life changer he wanted? The idea of moving to Wales had been strong enough to have the old farmhouse that he had bought and completely renovated using the local labour force. The entire project took nearly two years to complete. Mind you, he was in no rush to complete it. Now it was a very comfortable family residence. The building itself was situated a good five hundred metres off the main A5 road, eight miles further from Llangollen, in a village called Bonwm, *if you could call a dozen houses and farms stretched over a two-mile length of road a village.* The long drive up to the property, which curved slightly upwards and slightly round to the left, rendered the entire structure hidden from view of both the road and any other buildings, not that there were many about. There were also two stone barns within the curtilage. Those were still barns; he had thought of making them into holiday lets, but the Welsh frowned on such things. The grounds included a dozen or more huge trees as well as many smaller ones, with a stream running to one side. Large hedges surrounded it and, in all, stood on about 35 acres. What he had paid for the entire project wouldn't buy a garage where he was living now.

So, after much consideration and deliberation, Martin had taken the plunge and decided to retire and move to this property in North Wales. This would require selling his house in Surrey and moving his entire personal belongings to that part of the country. He had worked out his finances, which, although not enormous, would keep him in a certain lifestyle without having to worry too much about any nasty bills. His hobby wasn't lavish, but drawing, painting, and going on walks to accomplish both. He was happy to sit for hours painting and or drawing gnarled old trees with their roots growing over misshapen rocks, or old stone barns with their roofs falling in, even old gates and posts not touched for years, and nowhere was more suited to these types of subjects than North Wales.

Martin had never known his mother; she had died while giving birth to Martin. His father had died when Martin was twenty-one from a heart attack, one he never recovered from. His father was not a particularly communicative person and probably pined for his wife, which Martin thought he never really got over. Consequently, his father never told him of any other family members, which he had always thought a little strange, if not quite bizarre. Most people had cousins unless they had been adopted, which was something he had considered, which may have happened to him. That last remark was difficult to believe as Martin had looked just like his father; both he and his father were six feet tall, with a fairly large nose and high forehead, not particularly handsome but a likable and amiable character that neither man ever lost their temper or raised their voices, he was also a quiet and a very private person, also solivagant and quite happy in his own company.

It took nearly six months for Martin to wrap up his business dealings with his old company, sell his house in Surrey, and move into the Farmhouse. He also sold his Lexus, which was his pride and joy at the time, and bought a new Suzuki four-wheel drive. He thought it was a car, not too ostentatious but correct for the weather and terrain in this area. It had now been a few weeks since he moved, and he was now settling into a daily routine in this Welsh farmhouse. He didn't know why, but he bought a new large chest freezer from Curry's in Wrexham; the only thing in it was a few bits from Iceland.

The downside to everything was that it was now October, he knew it rained more in Wales, but the weather was turning much colder, and he wasn't sure if that was normal, he hadn't yet acclimatised himself, or it was generally colder than he thought this time of year, and he had never noticed it before.

The only other additional encumberment, or was it an additional part of Welsh life, was a black cat. It had appeared the second day he arrived there, soaking wet and looking very sorry for itself, that it seemed to think Martin was a soft touch. Unfortunately, he fed the animal, and that was enough to seal the fate of the two of them, as he seemed to move in, allowing Martin to also live beside him, rather than the other way around, but ground rules were defined, the cat was named Raffles, he was allowed into the utility room where he would quite happily lay on top of the oil boiler; which Martin had put a thick old towel on top and go to sleep after having a good preening session, and something Martin was uncomfortable about was the amount of attention he gave to his arse.

Martin had planned his first outing in this new surrounding area, not that it needed planning, but as he had been planning both his work and, naturally, his leisure time his entire life, this was a difficult habit to get out of. Having obtained the latest Ordnance Survey maps a few days before, he had studied them with care and wondered not for the first time that, wherever an area he planned to go, it was always on a joint over two maps. The area he had first chosen to go to was basically at the rear of Martin's property, but not readily accessible from just there. Although there were old pathways going out, he never thought he would try them, as he didn't know if he was trespassing. There was a so-called mountain range in the distance behind him called the Berwyn. This range was really only very steep, large hills, with the top being over 800 metres at the highest point. Martin had no intention of going that high or that far, but there were large outcrops of steep rocks along the way, with both deciduous and evergreen trees, which were in the guise of fir and Oak trees, all at the lower end, which should make interesting drawings and paintings.

According to the map, it was to these foothills and the outcrop of the rock formation that started there; he wanted to get to and explore. Martin would have to drive a short distance along the main road, and then, according to the map, there was a turning to the left with the unmistakable dotted lines of a track leading towards where he wanted to go.

As it was a glorious, bright, sunny day and the rain had stopped for the time being, he packed a few things into a knapsack containing all his painting equipment, some sandwiches, a flask of coffee, and other bits and pieces, and set off. It only took a short while before he arrived at the track marked on his map. He parked his car at the mouth of this track, tucking it well into the side to allow any other vehicles to pass. He wasn't sure whether it was a public track or not. In fact, he was not sure whether he should be walking there.

He hoisted the small knapsack onto his back and set off toward this so-called mountain range. He had been walking for over 20 minutes on a steady incline on this remote track, wondering why other people didn't come to this beautiful area more, stopping every now and then to look around the stunning scenery. At the end of the now muddy track, there seemed to be others crossing it, another barely noticeable one running across like a 'T' junction. There were massive rock outcrops with a fast-flowing stream cascading down to one side. The trees looked as if they grew out of the rocks themselves, and he noticed there were many different types of moss growing on the rocks and the trees, thick moss many inches thick, which also covered the ground. It was like walking on a mattress. He came across what looked like yet another track crossing the track he was now on. It was also starting to get far steeper. Martin decided this track had been made by animals such as foxes and not by humans, as he had first thought. After a short time, he stopped for a coffee break and sketched a gnarled old oak tree in which the roots that covered the rock it was sitting on looked as if they grew out of the rock itself. Using graphite pencils on a type of paper that gave him a satisfying result, he drew all the twisted and contorted roots and bark, with the odd bracken and moss around the base. After a short while, he looked at his picture and was quite pleased, then looking around him, he realised he was totally contented, wishing he had moved to Wales years ago.

Martin put away all his equipment and continued this fairly steep climb, going this way and that. After about another half an hour, he came across what can only be described as a sheer rock face. Looking around to see if there was any way around it before having to turn back the way he had come, he noticed what could only be described as steps. They were steep and covered in moss and looked as if they had been hewn out of the rock itself, but he was struggling to believe anyone would carve out steps in this remote part of the British Isles; the thickness of some of the moss covering these steps was indicative of not having been used for many years. He gradually made his way up these steps, which were both slippery and steep, pushing the moss off each step as he went, as he knew coming down would be more difficult.

He eventually came out at the top of these steps onto a plateau overlooking virtually the entire Dee Valley, and the view was quite breathtaking, with the river Dee snaking through the valley. He could also make out parts of the heritage railway that ran from Llangollen to Corwen that would carry passengers who enjoyed the old steam locomotives; he would have a ride himself one day. Removing his knapsack, he decided lunch was well overdue and decided to sit with his back to the rock face, looking and admiring this fantastic view, trying to identify certain areas he could see.

Within seconds of sitting down against the rock, it felt like the entire mountain was moving. Quickly grabbing his belongings, he stood up and ran to the edge of the plateau. Looking about him at what had just occurred, he couldn't detect anything that had altered or moved. After a few moments, he walked back to where he had been sitting, trying to understand not so much the noise, which was very little, but the feeling that something had moved, and failing to detect anything. He was not quite sure what to do after that particular experience. In fact, he doubted if he could explain the experience. In the end, he placed his hand on the rock to see if it was loose, which was ridiculous as it was 5 metres high and must have weighed as many tonnes. But as he did so, there was a feeling of movement in his hand, and the entire rock face started to vibrate and move. Martin stepped back in absolute amazement just as this massive rock slowly crept to one side. It never slid. It never rolled. It just moved a good metre and a half to one side to reveal a gaping hole.

Martin stood there for some moments, his mouth wide open, not knowing what to think. After a few minutes, he tried to peer into the very black hole before remembering his mobile smartphone had a light on it. He dived into the knapsack, produced his device, and switched the light on, not knowing whether to go in or not for fear it would close once inside. Throwing caution to the wind and intrigued by what had just happened, he advanced into the cave. It opened up into a large 5 metre more-or-less square room that appeared to have been cut out of the slate, which is now what he knew to be the material making up all these rocks. This was obviously the opening to a slate mine, but as he thought of that, he also considered how the devil would they get the slate down all those steep steps once it had been extracted. That was silly. They must have gone over the top, but there could have been another opening, of course. Whatever they say about Welsh slate and the saying of 'covering the roofs of the world,' the amount of slate making up this mountain, he wouldn't be at all surprised.

Chapter Two

He shone the small but quite bright light from his mobile around as he advanced further into the entrance; he was reviewing what he first thought of as a mine entrance. This was what now looked very much like a cave. A large mound was set in the centre of the room near the entrance, then as he glanced around saw what looked like a bench down one wall, both items were built in slate by their appearance, although it was difficult to tell as everything was covered in thick dust and cobwebs, so-much-so it was inches thick, in the far corner there was what could be a fireplace, at one time there must have been a chimney, or at least a hole in the ceiling, as greenery was growing all up the wall and past the ceiling, to where water had trickled down. The opposite corner was another hole cut through the slate; on approaching, discovered it led into another smaller room. A much smaller room with a structure some half a metre off the floor stretched across one side, he thought this must be the bedroom, again so thick with cobwebs and dust, and as Martin didn't want to touch anything, not because it was dirty, more that he felt as if he was intruding on someone's private place.

He returned to the main room and approached this bench, for want of another word. With a sweep of his hand, he removed some of the cobwebs, pushing them onto the floor, and continued removing this debris with a piece of metal he found leaning against the wall. In the centre of the bench, once the rubbish was cleared, was what looked like a very large book, so big he didn't realise it was a book. Now being far more careful, he pulled any other detritus that still remained from off the giant tome with his hands; it was pretty revolting. The top of this book was covered with what looked like a very thick piece of leather, he folded it back as carefully as he could, but it came away in his hands, this piece of covering had protected whatever was under it, for however long it had remained there, he noticed that the leaves of the book were all of varying in size, the edges all brown but there was writing, he tried to study it, but as he did so started to think; how much life was left in the battery of his phone, so he carefully replaced the leather cover back on the book and exited the cave.

He stood outside the entrance of this cave for some time, thinking, whilst looking around at this magnificent view: what little heat there was in the sun had now faded. He decided to finish his sandwiches and coffee off, but his hands were filthy, holding the corner of the bread by the plastic bag he wrapped them in, while also reflecting on what he had just discovered. Who would have lived up here in this isolated part of the British Isles, if that's what anybody had done? Martin knew, in the 17th and 18th centuries, that Lords of the manors, who owned vast estates, had ornamental hermits living in caves as well as small shacks to amuse and entertain their visitors, but no visitors would get up here, not easily anyhow. And then another thought came to him: why did the entrance open the way it did? He inspected this massive piece of slate that had covered the cave entrance, tried to push and pull at it, it was only like pushing a brick house it must weigh 5 or 6 tonnes, the only thing he could think of was, it must have been on a stone or something similar and toppled off it just at that moment, improbable but that's all he could think of at this moment.

Replacing his knapsack on his back and a quick look round, he started back for home, leaving the gap wide open, thinking and deeply puzzled. He was now going back down these steps extremely slowly, but it was halfway down when he heard a low rumble, and was now even more curious, especially if what he suspected, the stone had gone back into position, but had to dismiss that thought as totally absurd. On the way back to his home along these small tracks, he bent small pieces of twigs and laid them on the track, just to make sure he would be able to find the route again.

When he entered his house, he was greeted with a sort of half-hearted meow, and realised he needed two things: a cat flap in the door and food for the cat.

The following day, Martin was still thinking of the

mysterious happenings on that plateau the day before; in fact, could think of little else. So, he again grabbed his knapsack as before, but this time included torches and spare batteries, and as an afterthought, a small brush; his drawing equipment had remained there. A fresh flask of coffee and more sandwiches, he enjoyed his sandwiches, albeit they usually had the same fillings.

So, after topping up Raffles' food bowl with some choice pieces of leftover pilchards he had for tea a couple of days earlier, promising the cat he would get him some proper food later on, he set off.

It was a far nicer day than yesterday; the sun was warming up nicely. He parked his car where he had the day before and set out for the cave again. First, by the more prominent track that had probably been there for centuries, and almost missing one of the turnings he had marked out, but he eventually arrived at the base of the steps. There were 44 steps to the top; he counted them, but when he arrived, the stone was back in place. "Bugger," he said aloud, wondering how the hell something as big and as heavy as that could possibly move back to its original position. So, sitting down with his back to the entrance again to admire the view, and ponder what would make a six-tonne stone move on its own. No sooner had he sat down than the massive lump of slate moved to one side exactly like it had the previous day, still making him jump backwards, which was even more puzzling than the day before. Cautiously, he entered the cave with possibly more trepidation than the day before, wondering if this place had a mind of its own. Turning on his torch, which he had removed from his knapsack, and again peering around this cave with a lot more light this time. The lump in the centre of the room was a table of sorts made up of slate. There was little else one could say about it. Then continued glancing around the room to see what else was in there. He discovered a large pestle and mortar tucked into one corner. At the side of this was what must have been definitely a fire, which he thought yesterday; he pulled off some of the green algae and other things that looked like ferns growing, which had accumulated over many years, how many years he had absolutely no idea.

He moved over to look more closely at what must be a bench, taking out the small brush, he had packed, and clearing all the cobwebs along with the accumulated dust off its entire length. Clouds of dust bellowed out everywhere. Martin retreated outside to wait until the dust settled, pouring himself a cup of coffee while he waited.

When he next entered, the amount of rubbish now amassed on the floor was unbelievable, but the top was looking better to reveal the treatise he had tried to look at the previous day, it dominated most of the top where it was situated, before he looked at this massive tome he decided to look about the place now with a far better light, also taking out his rucksack a battery lantern which would stand on any flat surface, he entered what he thought may have been a bedroom, placing the lantern on the floor in the centre of the room to inspect the low structure tucked away in one side, was it a bed? Only to quickly realise there was a skeleton stretched out on top of it. Martin jumped back, but then was quickly aware it was probably 300 years old, or even older. Anything more than that would surely have rotted away. Also, it seemed to have some sort of covering over it, which may have been a blanket, but would a blanket last that long?

Leaving the macabre alone, he returned back to the main room to take a better look at the book, it was then he noticed a row of stone jars on a sort of ledge let into the slate walls, all the stone jars were of different shapes and sizes, he picked one out and placed it on the bench, it must have had a leather top of some kind but that had all perished, however, somebody had written with either ink or paint onto the stone jar itself, he could tell there was writing but hadn't a clue what it said, he decided to copy what was there onto paper, he grabbed some paper and a pencil out of his bag. He copied it down exactly as it had been written, more importantly, how it had been written. He took down some of the other jars and did the same thing to all of them.

He then turned his attention to the book itself. Once again, carefully removing by turning over the large, thick piece of leather covering not only the top, but this piece of leather was big enough to hang down over the sides, which had protected it from the elements. He would have liked to take the book home, but for one thing, it looked very heavy and cumbersome. For another, he didn't know who owned it, as it had been there for many years and had not come to any harm thus far.

Focusing on this giant tome he opened up to the first page, small squiggly writing stretched all across the page which was not only illegible but was obviously written in a totally different era to what Martin understood, turning the page it was much the same, so he took a handful of these sheets turned them over so not to mix them up; the page he was now looking at, was more akin to a page of writing albeit nothing he could understand. Then, he spent the next hour copying what was written down exactly as he could make out; there were many strange markings above and below the letters, a bit like accents but far more flowing. After quite some time bending in the same position, he realised he was now very stiff as his back was aching, so he went outside to straighten his back and have another coffee. After throwing the dregs away, he went back and copied some more pages; all the writing was totally alien to him, but somebody would surely know what was written down. He was about to pack up all his equipment, and was just inspecting all the sheets that made up this book more closely, he was no expert but it looked like lots of joined sheets made into one great big one, well joined where they touched as the bindings had all but disintegrated, which made the whole book dangerously fragile; he was putting the tome back together when he came across a sheet with very few words on, but what was there made his eyes open wide and the hairs on his back stand out, but then never-the-less went on to copy down exactly as it was written, **Myrddin**, that had been crossed out and **Merlinus** had been substituted, there was a date beneath, Martin's hand was shaking as he wrote it down **LCCXXVII.** That date didn't make sense since this book couldn't be that old, but he couldn't argue with what was written down, and it certainly didn't look like any forgery; this needed double-checking when he got home.

Martin had been so absorbed in his work that he hadn't noticed the time—no wonder he was starving; it was already past three. He definitely didn't want to be heading down that mountain after dark. With a very aching back, he quickly packed everything away and started back immediately. On the way down the steps, the same rumbling was heard.

He thought this was getting to be silly, especially if that rock had closed on its own again. Once back home, he was excited to know what everything meant in all that writing. What also excited him more than anything was the name and, specifically, the date in the book; if it was correct, all previous myths and legends would be thrown out the window. But a persistent meowing was now weaving itself around his legs, wanting to be fed, and he still had no food for the cat.

Chapter Three

Martin ate his dinner in earnest, clearing everything away from his dining table, not even bothering to wash up. With mounting excitement, he got out all the papers he had been busily scribbling away at in the cave. He fired up his computer and typed in the first name **Myrddin,** Welsh for Merlin, and probably the author's original name. The next was **Merlinus,** which was the Latin version of Merlin. So far, so good, which he had half expected.

Until now, he thought the story of Merlin was nothing more than that, a story, embellished over many decades, especially with the fictitious Arthurian connection. These stories were started way back in 1136 by Geoffrey of Monmouth's Historia Regum Britanniae. It was believed that Geoffrey had based Merlin on a blend of earlier historical and legendary figures, some of whom may never have existed at all. On top of that, Geoffrey had written three different versions of the stories, spaced out over a number of years, all variations on the same theme, all with subtle differences, making them seem individual.

Once he had put the name Merlin into his computer it came up with several theories, some in abundance about

Merlin, one is of a North Brythonic Prophet, another a 5th Century person called Merlinus Caledonensis, and yet another Myrddin Wyllt, translated from Welsh as Merlin the Wild, Martin had dismissed all those as being either the wrong years or just too fanciful. It was the last name that came up unexpectedly on his computer, **Merlinus Ambrosins,** making Martin sit up and take more notice. He realised the similarity to his own name as well as that of a so-called long-dead myth, which were extremely similar, **Martin Ambrose - Merlin Ambrosins.** He dismissed any thought of being a distant relative as totally and utterly absurd.

Next, the date was far more significant. **L = 500, C = 100, X = 10.** If you add these with their multiples, so the L is 500, then 2 x 100, 2 x 10, and 2 x 11 equate to **722.** Was this possible? Was this the date when the first sheet was ascribed? If you take into account the number of cobwebs and accumulated dust all around, he thought it was possibly that old.

So, if it was started in 722, when was it finished? If you believe all the stories about Merlin, he lived for hundreds of years, and was that Merlin in the bed? Surely bones don't last for 1300 years, let alone the cloth which was still on the skeleton, still more questions, and as yet, not many answers to any of them. The trouble was that the more he thought about it, the deeper it was going; those papers/parchments had been started in Anno Domini 722, so the finished or last entry was anybody's guess.

The writings on the bottles/jars had no accents above the writing. He entered those directly into his computer, using the translation from Latin to English. He was always told that Latin was a dead language; he would soon discover how dead it was. The first one was **Mus Dentes,** translated to Mouse teeth. Next, **canis lupus ossibus,** fox cub bones. **Lupos cor meum,** Wolf heart. After a few more of these gruesome animal body parts, he got the picture, and what they would be used for was subject to conjecture. So, it was down to the book or piles of parchments that went into making up that book. So far, Martin had only looked up odd words; this was a totally different kettle of fish. He needed somebody who knew Latin well. If indeed it was Latin, there must be far more to Latin than he ever thought possible. Maybe there was Old English mixed in with this writing, or even Welsh; is there ancient Welsh? Martin thought he needed help, but who did he ask? And, more importantly, how do you ask somebody and not get them involved? How was he to find such a scholar, even if one did exist?

Time was getting late; he closed his computer, put away all the paperwork, and made himself a drink. He sat back and mused over what had happened over the last two days, the stone that moved, the skeleton, the book, the bottles, the table, and the pestle and mortar, would all that conjure up a wizard? Was there even such a thing? Martin, until that moment, would have dismissed it without even thinking about it, but it was there, it wasn't a dream, I doubt if any of that could be faked, he thought, and why would anyone want to fake it anyway? He still couldn't accept any reasonable explanation for the stone moving, or even more puzzling, why and how the stone knew when to return to its original position? Lastly, the skeleton was old, that was for sure, but how old was it, and why were the remains of the sheet still covering the skeleton, even if there was little left of it? There were far too many questions, and none that could be answered without even more questions being asked.

Martin went to sleep later, before he dropped off; his head was still in a spin, amongst all the questions, the biggest one of all was, who was he? Where was the rest of my family? He knew he had no siblings, but there must be uncles, aunts, cousins, and far more besides somewhere, surely?

The following day, Martin was thinking about his father, also named Martin. When his father had died, he had put everything he owned into storage through Pickfords. (All he had actually done was make one phone call; everything else was done for him. It was even better and quicker than taking everything to the tip.) They had packed it, boxed it, and taken it into storage. All Martin had done was set up a standing order to pay for the storage. He distinctly remembered some tea chests, as well as rugs, furniture, beds; he shuddered to think what else was there, and had never had the heart to throw anything away. Now was the time he thought to go and collect it out of storage and bring it all to Wales, nearly 30 years after it had been originally stored.

He organised and hired a large vehicle from a local company the following day and went off to Leicestershire to reclaim his father's house contents, following a phone call he had made beforehand to the company that owned the storage facility. When they opened the container, it stunk. He offered two of the men a large tip if they could help him split the load in two; one for rubbish to be taken and deposited to the local tip, another to take back to Wales with him, for one thing, he would not get all these contents in one lorry load.

It was getting very late when Martin was driving through Llangollen, some eight miles from his home, he decided to get some fish and chips from a shop on the main road, then put them under the heater to keep warm till pulling into a lay-by just up the road. He sat and ate them out of the polystyrene container, wondering why it is that they always taste better when eaten outside. He arrived back at the old farmhouse with the lorry; he was too tired to unload that night, he realised how unfit he was, and the money he gave the men to help him load up was worth every penny. He also realised that he had still not brought any food for the cat, which seemed content sitting on the boiler, licking his backside with one of his legs stuck up in the air. Martin wondered if he had found his own fur or feathered supper from outside. After making himself a drink, he went straight to bed and slept.

The following morning was spent at his new home in Wales. It seemed he was enjoying being there more than anywhere else. It was raining, thankfully not torrential rain, but that horrible constant drizzle that seems to soak everything. He unloaded the van's contents by backing up the van as close to the barn doors as possible, where he was to temporarily store everything. Thankfully, all the furnishings and white goods he had taken to the tip, he was now left with mainly all the boxes, just in the hope that it might reveal something of his family. Why he hadn't disposed of it all instead of hanging onto them in the first place, Martin had no idea whatsoever. He returned the lorry to its owners, picking up his car simultaneously, and then drove home. Once there, he started tackling his father's and his family's remaining lives out of all the boxes.

He stood there looking about wondering which box to tackle first, with a Stanley knife in hand he undid the first, it was full of drinking glasses as well as other wrapped up fragile receptacles, the next was full of ornaments and the third full of pictures and photo's, the fourth was much more promising, piles of papers, whether any good or not he would find out soon enough; he pulled that particular tea chest over to the house. The next two boxes were full of blankets and sheets; the last box had all sorts of bits and pieces in it, and what looked like a black bag filled with letters and other written material. He dragged that over to the house as well. Then, he made himself a cup of coffee and started going through years of nothing more than what appeared at first to be rubbish. There were old guarantees, old bank statements, cheque book stubs, and even instructions to assemble an MFI wardrobe. He did find some solicitor letters, and what looked like legal documents which were all tied up together, he put them all to one side, he would look at them later and continued to riffle through the rest of the chest's contents, saving a few items and putting them also to one side, then bundled everything back into the tea chest and replaced it back into the barn. Once a week, the council refuge collectors brought their small wagon into the yard. The two lads who came were exceptionally helpful and would almost certainly take the lot; what they did with it all was up to them.

Raffles had decided he wanted to help and came into the dining room to see what on earth was going on. The cat took a couple of sniffs at all the accumulated rubbish and decided it had nothing to do with him, so he started to go in and out of his legs again. Martin realised he hadn't been fed, so he had to stop what he was doing and organise food for the cat.

The last box he had dragged across to the house appeared to be full of bits of everything. He systematically went through the lot. There was another bag of papers, a few odds and ends he thought might be useful, but the most important find yet lay at the bottom. It was what looked like a very old wooden box, approximately 400 millimetres square. It had a leather strap wrapped around it and was held together with an intricate lock. He lifted it clear from the bottom of the chest and placed it on the kitchen table. He had not seen a key of any kind. After all this time, the chances of finding it were pretty remote. He selected a sharp knife from the kitchen drawer and cut through the leather band. It was a bit rash, but Martin was intrigued by what was in this wooden box. What made it more intriguing was that he never recalled ever having seen it when he was younger.

Once inside the box, it was obviously recognisable as the Ambrose family tree. The last name written on the top sheet of paper was his fathers, Martin Grey Ambrose, born 15th April 1939, this must have been written by his grandfather, probably shortly after his father had been born, it was a shame his father hadn't also been so enthusiastic, as he may have found out a bit more of his mother and her family. His grandfather had married an Isabelle Ruth Longs; their dates of birth, marriage, and deaths were all recorded. His great-grandfather was also Martin Grey Ambrose, so was his father before him; this monotony of names for the oldest male went back through many years and many sheets of paper. Martin also realised there were either very few siblings or they hadn't been recorded; the majority of the time, there was only one son recorded. The further back in years he looked, the size of the paper changed, as did the material it was written on. Then, in 1551, different names started to appear. The name Martin changed to Martyn, then Mervyn, and there was a Mosyn and even a Mayn. The Grey middle name disappeared back in the 18th Century. The further back in the box he went, the older the parchment was, but the family tree kept going back in time.

As Martin removed the last handful of sheets out of the box, he thought it must be one of the finest historical descendant family trees in Britain. The last sheets looked extremely delicate; Martin took tremendous care not to damage any of the last parchments. The last few pieces were difficult to decipher but there on the last but one, on the top of the page, it was faded but quite legible **Myrddin** born 708 wife Olwyn, there were other siblings mentioned but most of the names were unpronounceable, on the last page more names and dates but the ravages of time had removed most of them, the family name of Ambrose had changed just before 1200 from Ambrosins.

Martin sat back, his back ached, his head ached, and his stomach was rumbling; he was drained and exhausted. But the truth of the matter was, he **was** a direct descendant of Merlin, Martin had no idea what that might imply, not all dates had been written in, especially some of the deaths which included Merlin's, why that was he had no idea, and probably never would, but there again if he had died in that cave then nobody else would know other than his wife, he may have outlived her by a hundred years for all Martin knew.

Chapter Four

It had been 2 o'clock in the morning by the time Martin had gone to bed after eating a very late supper. He had a surprisingly good night's sleep, waking quite refreshed at nearly 10 o'clock. Letting the cat outside, which was now becoming the norm. Then, cooked eggs, bacon, and toast for a brunch, while he was eating, he was pondering again about everything he had learnt, and what he was going to do about it. The biggest question of all was whether it was because he was related to Merlin that the front of the cave opened, and he wondered if other relations, no matter how distant, could also move that slate door, or if indeed anybody else could move it.

It was all very well knowing you are a descendant of the most famous mythical legend in history, but what do you do with that information, especially when you don't have any aspirations to perform magic? In fact, he could barely shuffle a pack of cards. Then another thought flashed into his mind: did any of his past relations know about the cave, or even that they were related to this famous ancestor? That was simple to answer. No, that cave had not been entered since the person lying in that bed had died, that he was quite sure about.

So, to the next question, was the skeleton Merlin? If it was, could those bones be 1300 years old? He would need an anthropologist to tell him that. However, maybe the cloth could give him a clue. Next question: Should he tell somebody in authority about it? He would, but not just yet. The secret has been kept for so long; a little longer would make no difference. So Martin decided to leave that particular scenario at least as the status quo. He then had a sudden thought about his ancestral lineage. If he didn't have a son, the line would be broken. Maybe that could be rectified, but so far it had not been put to the test, and he hoped he had not left it too late.

After he had washed up and cleared everything away, and as it was now pouring with rain, he decided to have a closer look at the old wooden box the family tree had been kept in. The papers/parchments were still piled up in the same order as they came out of the box, and were still in the middle of the dining table. The box itself was old but definitely not classed as ancient; the insides were covered in what looked like white silk, although the material was coming away from the sides in most places. He turned the whole thing upside down and gave it a shake. There were plenty of small particles of paper and parchments falling out, but also two small keys, which he put to one side. He replaced everything carefully back into the box exactly as he had found it. He was now sorry to have cut the leather strap; he would get that repaired without too much difficulty. The two keys were totally different from each other, one about 50 mm long including its handle, the other much smaller, both looked like brass but could just as easily be gold, one certainly looked like any old fashioned type, and could be, err, he was thinking how long keys of that type had been made 150 years old, maybe a little older, but the other could barely be called a key, for a start he thought the key wards and bit that are on all keys had been broken off, but further inspection revealed it to have a cylindrical blade, it was like a key he had never seen before and no idea what either key opened. They certainly wouldn't open anything in the cave, and they definitely wouldn't have opened this wooden box. Before doing anything else, he placed the box with all the ancestry sheets at the bottom of the airing cupboard.

Once he had put everything else away, he opened his computer and searched the Internet for scholars in ancient Latin/Old English. Celtic languages, he came across two, ironically, one in Oxford, the other in Cambridge. He sent them both a sample of what he had copied down from the book through an email, asking both how much they would charge to decipher a manuscript of similar material, going on to say that this manuscript had recently come into his possession. He outlined some of the difficulties he had copying it out on a computer, as an explanation for the attachment to go with the missive.

He had gone as far as he could with explanations of

all the pieces of writing, so he got ready for a longer expedition to the cave. He intended to copy as much down from the book as he could; each page seemed to take ages, as there were so many accents above many of the letters as well as below, also many squiggles, he had no idea what they were, they could even be the author's doodling, and there were hundreds of them. He had a small Sony camera with a 32 GB memory; he didn't want to use his mobile as he didn't trust the internet, and at the moment, he certainly did not want anything other than what he had copied down and sent to those people going onto the web. He was also reticent about taking anything from the cave other than cobwebs and dust, and photographs. Then, as an afterthought, he also took some small sealable plastic containers, along with a copious amount of paper, pens, and pencils. Then went and did a bit of shopping, mainly for the cat, and wondered if the mouse-flavoured meat inside the tins it had said it contained had anything to do with a mouse.

The following morning, it was drizzling again, so waterproofs as well as everything else were the order of the day. He put his knapsack in the boot, having filled it with his usual comestibles as well as everything else he had prepared the night before, and set off in his car the short distance to where he had parked on previous occasions.

As he travelled along the road, he realised there was no arable farming around here, mainly sheep with a few cattle thrown in for good measure. He was unsure why exactly that was, but thought it could be, as there was little good soil. He had just parked, got out of his car, and started to remove his rucksack from the back when a tractor trundled around the corner and stopped at the side of him. The driver got out of his cab and walked over. "Hello," Martin said in his friendliest manner he could adopt. "I hope you don't mind me leaving my car just here?"

"Well, this is all private land. Where have you come from?" he asked in that lovely sing-song voice that the Welsh have.

"I bought the old farm a short distance away a few years back. I have just retired and settled in, now I'm just looking around the area."

"Would that be old Gwian's farm?"

"Do you know, I think that was his Christian name, a Mr. Williams."

"Then we are neighbours, my name is Evan Griffiths," and he stuck his muddy hand out, which Martin readily shook.

"My name is Martin Ambrose. How many acres do you farm?" Martin asked conversationally, and to sound interested and knowledgeable.

"I own about 700, but farm over a thousand, mainly sheep, but I have a few cattle as well. I was going to buy the old property myself, that stream behind the old farmhouse has never known to dry up, sometimes I could do with that water, especially in hot summers."

"Well, I have no intention of keeping any animals, other than a cat that seems to have adopted me. Maybe we can come to some agreement, say, for the swap of the odd lamb joint for the freezer, in exchange for water anytime you want it." Then Martin continued. "Who owns all the land up there?" pointing the way he was facing and up into the mountain.

"I own up to the outcrop, which includes the track running along the base, that track used to be the main thoroughfare into Corwen before the A5 was built, Owain Glyndwr owned all the land around here in the day, it's had many owners since then, the Forestry Commission look after the trees but nobody really wants the land you can't even keep sheep up there, not if you want to keep them alive." He replied easily and then asked. "Going back to what you just said about the water, that my friend is the best offer I have had for some time," he said with a big grin. "Come up to the house when you have time, and meet the wife," he stuck his hand out again and added. "Put your car further up the lane, it will be safer there, you can leave it anytime you like." Martin thanked him and told him he would come over sometime next week. Then returned to his car and moved it further up the lane, where indicated. Pulled his rucksack onto his back and set off back to the cave. When he eventually arrived there and before he touched the rock, he looked closely at how well it disguised the cave. With the exception of some crushed vegetation along the floor, there was no way you would know there was a cave behind it. As before, he placed his hand on the rock and, like before, it neither shuddered nor rumbled; it just moved, the ground vibrated a bit, but that was because a few tonnes of rock were on the move. He turned on his torches and entered. The first task was to remove a small sample of cloth from the skeleton. He thought he would be able to just pick a piece up; it was lucky he had brought a small pair of scissors with him, and he was able to cut a small portion and put it into one of the sealed plastic containers. There would be no way to pull it apart without destroying it. Then, he took a good look around the bedroom. He looked at the skeleton, knowing now it was almost certain to be one of his ancestors; the rest contained nothing more than what looked like rubbish, in-so-much as it had not survived the ravages of time.

Returning to the main room, and opening the book back to the position he had got to, then for no reason he turned to about a third of the way through, placed his own papers to the right of the book so he was able to write down on the work surface, settling the light immediately above. So, with the decent light illuminating the area, started copying down exactly as it had been written all those years before, squiggle for squiggle, line for line and this time taking special attention to all the small accents and other symbols both above and below the words that he may have missed before, what they did or what they represented he hadn't a clue. Once he had completed this first page of Merlin's book, which took two of his own, he put a tiny pencil mark at the bottom of the page, and a '1', then put a '1' on each of his own pages. He straightened up and went out into the rain to have a cup of coffee. He enjoyed just looking at the view, wondering how much of it had changed since Merlin was alive. He copied out five more pages, each one demanding intense focus and time. Accuracy mattered more to him than speed. The text contained nothing resembling modern language, yet now and then, a word seemed vaguely familiar. As he continued copying, a distinct ethos began to emerge from the script. Intermittently, he ate sandwiches and cake and drank his coffee. He cleaned all the cobwebs and rubbish, along with the greenery where the fire had been. This was not to make it habitable but to see what else was in there, discovering some very strange implements in the corners, all of metal. Whether the wood part of the implement had rotted, leaving just metal, he had no idea. Along with metal, there were what would have been mountains of parchments, all now completely useless, and any writing had long disappeared. He took a few photos, looked and inspected every detail in the cave. What couldn't escape his mind was *what on earth Merlin ate when living up here?* Did he have snares all about to catch animals? Did he venture out to some shop of some sort? All that paled into insignificance. It seemed to be all down to the writing on the parchments, which Martin had called a book. There were no other clues who had lived there, no matter what they were or did, Martin thought now, after inspecting everything inside this cave, Merlin was nothing more than a scribe, but what those scribbled notes revealed, or even what he hoped it would reveal there was no telling, but something might just tell him more about his long dead relative. Which, on the face of it, he was finding out more about Merlin than he knew about his own father, or any other member of his family, come to think of it.

Chapter Five

As he set off back to his home, the rain was now coming down in torrents, making the steps slippery as well as slightly dangerous, but at least his car was now much nearer.

Once back at his house, the cat was waiting expectantly outside the door and soaking wet. Martin filled his bowl; he had purchased a mouse-flavoured food from the local shop and left him to it. While his supper was cooking, he downloaded all the pictures he had taken from inside the cave and put them all onto a USB stick, then ensured any trace of the photos was deleted from his camera, leaving no trace anywhere, as he was petrified of someone hacking into this so-called modern technology. He then opened the small plastic container with the remnants of the cloth he had removed from the skeleton. Inspecting it more closely under a strong light and a magnifying glass, it was now obvious why it was difficult to pull apart - there was something akin to thin metal threads running through it, surely the only material around then which would have stood the test of time

and possibly remain pliable would be gold. The skeleton would now almost certainly be Merlin. If, indeed, Merlin had worn such an item of clothing, maybe he only wore it to die in; now that's a sobering thought.

Once dinner was eaten and cleared away, he then looked at his computer to see if anyone had sent him an email regarding his inquiry: Bingo, a Professor Stone from Cambridge University.

It read:

Hi Mr. Ambrose

I am a professor of ancient languages. I have deciphered most of the words from the text you have sent, although the text is insufficient in detail. However, what you enclosed for me to decipher is extremely interesting, as well as intriguing, as to where it may have come from. Because of the nature and subject matter you sent, as well as the way you have indicated there may be more, I would very much like to meet with you to discuss a way in which we can both benefit. I feel I must add that if these papers are original and of an age indicated by their very wording, they should be in the British Museum. In any event, please contact me by email at your earliest convenience.'

– Professor C. Stone

Martin returned the email, telling the professor that, as he was now retired, they could name the time and place. Also, there were many more questions he needed answers to, and whether the answers were the correct metaphor.

Within minutes, the professor had replied, and made

arrangements to meet Martin the following Tuesday at midday, and suggested the Red Lion on the high street in Grantchester, not that far off the M11 and south of Cambridge, and to bring more of the same material with him.

So, on Monday, Martin got everything ready, including all the sheets he had copied, or rather the photocopied sheets of everything he had meticulously copied directly off Merlin's book, the original copies he stored in a box file and labelled insurance.

Ensuring he had a full tank of fuel, water to drink, biscuits to nibble, and entered the postcode of the Red Lion into his satnav. He was going to set off early as he wasn't sure how long the journey would take. He knew there was major roadwork at the junction of the M40 and the A14, but unfortunately, there was no way around them.

Before setting off, he put the cat's bowl of food inside one of the barns that he knew he could get into. He followed Martin in there anyway.

It was still dark when he set off, and nothing on the roads (there never is much in Wales at the best of times), a few lorries around Oswestry and not much more until he reached the gyratory around Birmingham. From then on, the traffic got more congested and consequently slower, especially going down the M6 and stop-start until he eventually reached the junction they were still building, where the M1 crosses and the A14 starts, taking over half an hour to travel 2 miles. Once through this traffic congestion, the rest of the way was not too bad, arriving an hour earlier than the agreed time, finding and parking his car in the car park opposite the Red Lion. The Red Lion was a newly thatched property that looked as if it had just had a makeover. He decided to stretch his legs and have a good walk through the Gratchester meadows and along the river Cam. It was a warm, bright day, but with a cool breeze. After taking in the delights of this river and never realising how many people had dogs, but nevertheless arriving back at the pub at exactly 12 o'clock. He strolled into the reception and asked the young lady behind the counter if anyone was waiting for him. He told her his name, and she confirmed that a Professor Stone was waiting for him in the restaurant.

He looked around when he entered the restaurant, and the only person in the restaurant stood up and walked towards him, "Mr. Ambrose," she said as she held her hand out to shake his.

A little taken aback, he replied. "Professor Stone, I presume?" She was only a fraction shorter than Martin, then he realised her heals were nearly a foot tall, she had an exceptionally attractive open face, very little make-up on and striking powder blue eyes, also what was termed as an hourglass figure; he had been half expecting a small white-bearded man in tweeds and a pair of glasses on the end of his bulbous little nose.

"Let's sit down and have something to eat, as I am

starving," she said as if they had known each other all their lives. "Call me Chloe. The salmon here is beautiful. I recommend that," so that is what they ordered. While they waited for their food to arrive and as the restaurant started filling up with lunchtime clientele, Chloe told Martin about her academic credentials and a little about herself and what she had studied, adding that she had a Master's in languages, studied and lectured in ancient tongues, and was extremely intrigued by the snippet he had sent her. "Have you any idea what it said? I sincerely hope you brought more for me to see. Where did you get it from? How did you come by it?"

Martin was at a complete loss as to which question to answer or if indeed she needed any of them answered. He had never been so bombarded with so many questions in such a short time, but before he could reply to any of her questions, their salmon arrived, and between mouthfuls, he replied while she had a mouthful of her own food, and thought he had to stem this assault of questioning. "One thing at a time, what did that piece say I sent to you? This salmon melts in the mouth, doesn't it?" he added.

As they were enjoying the food, neither said anything until they had finished eating; it had to be said that it was the most enjoyable food. Then the professor put her cutlery on the plate and moved the plate to one side, and after looking at Martin for a few seconds, she took a deep breath. "I am sorry, I get so excited and talk too much when something like the writing you sent me comes along. It doesn't happen very often. I can tell you that, in fact, it has never happened to me."

The waiter immediately picked up the cue to clear the table and ordered coffee, and Chloe produced a single sheet of paper from a briefcase and placed it on the table. "Did you copy this accurately?"

"Yes, but the light where I copied it was very poor. There could well be slight discrepancies; also, I had no knowledge of what I was copying down at the time. Most, if not all, the symbols in the texts aren't available on computers."

"And do you now have more knowledge of what you were copying on any subsequent pieces?" she asked with a furrowed brow.

"Let's say things have evolved since then. Why?"

"The piece you sent me, well, it's a sort of prophecy and doesn't make much sense on its own. How much more is there?"

"Volumes of it, I have brought some more for you to look at. I have the piece I copied out rather than a computer typeface, if that's any better?" and handed the piece of A4 paper over to her.

She took the proffered piece, studied the piece she had worked on, and wrote some notes on the paper Martin had given her. She was still not satisfied as she looked from one sheet to the other and then made some more slight adjustments.

Martin looked at the neat writing, just under the script

Martin had tried to copy out as best he could. He wasn't surprised in the least by what it said, and it must have shown on his face.

"You are not surprised," she said, picking up on his facial expressions.

"No, not in the slightest, but strange, to say in the least, that I should have chosen that particular piece for you to decipher. Why the brackets? Isn't it a straight translation?"

"In a word, no, but to even think you knew what was written, you must know when that piece was penned in the first place. Do you know how old that piece of writing is?"

"Yes, I do. Since I emailed that bit to you, I have discovered more of where it came from and possibly how it came to be where it is, and before you ask, I am not prepared to say where that is."

This is like getting blood out of a stone. For goodness' sake, Martin, tell me more. Can't you see? I'm very excited about this one little fragment you sent to me. However, I will tell you, if this were written 200 years ago, it would be silly. I am here because the accents on that fragment have not been used for well over three centuries, which then makes me both excited and nervous. If you have documents from before the 11th century, they should be in the British Museum. They will be jumping up and down if they find out you have something that is possibly 11th-century or older. Now, will you give me whatever you have or not?"

For an answer, he produced a pile of sheets and placed them in front of Chloe. She looked first at Martin, then down to the papers, picking up one and then another, and made a study of each. On the third sheet, she made notes, and for nearly ten minutes, she studied more of them intensely. The coffee had gone cold as she absentmindedly picked it up to drink, grimaced, and replaced the cup in the saucer. Then, suddenly, she looked up as if she had been in a trance and tried to justify her inattentiveness. "I can't just read it like a book. However, there are many words and passages I can read, and quite honestly, Martin, it's groundbreaking in what we know of early life in Britain," she picked up one sheet.

"This one, for instance, mentions Guthlac and why he went to Rome, which is not what we have been led to believe," then waved another couple of papers in the air. "These sheets talk of what is termed the Corvée, and this sheet mentions the Witan, which again is not what we know about it. In all, I must emphasise, Martin, the original documents need to go into the British Museum. They are extremely important, in fact, possibly the most important writing since Bede," she said, then she seemed to be bemused by that last statement. "Considering he only wrote about the ecclesiastical people of Britain, what you have here, from the little pieces I have seen, are events that actually happened, not just ministerial or religious. There are many things which are attached to either religion or, at the very least, indoctrination, which, in the past, we have guessed the outcomes, due mainly to what suits us, or more to the point, what may have suited the church, what you have, has thrown all that guesswork out of the window with proof positive, do you have the originals, and are they in a safe and secure place?"

Martin noticed she seemed very good at asking two questions, giving no room for an answer. "Yes and No."

She looked very hard at him for a better explanation. She realised she had not drunk her second coffee, which was also now cold, then remembered she had previously determined that and had asked for another, realising this man in front of her just sat patiently and waited for her next move.

"I own them, I suppose. I don't want to move them from where they are stored, and the land and the place where they are stored belong to someone else. I will add that they have been stored there since they were written, and it's extremely secure."

"Have you any idea how old the originals are?" she asked as if he wouldn't have a clue.

"They were started in about 722 AD," he said in a matter-of-fact way that she had now come to expect.

"Martin," she said slowly. "If what you are telling me is truthful, and I have no doubt it is, these would be the rarest parchments in history and definitely need to be preserved, not just secured. Would you trust me enough to show me where they are so I can see for myself? For something as important as this, I am totally at your disposal."

Martin sat for a while, contemplating what Chloe had just said. "You would have to come back to North Wales with me. I can tell you now that it's very difficult to take in; certain myths and legends go out the window, which I have come to find out myself over the past few weeks."

"Would you follow me back to my flat to get my computer and a change of clothes? Do I need to book into a hotel or have you a settee I can doss down on?"

"You can stay with me. I have a spare bedroom, and you will need more than a change of clothes, though. Do you have walking boots along with the rest of that type of outdoor attire?"

"Why do you live on a mountain?" she said with a grin.

"No, but where you will be going is."

"This is getting more intriguing as we go along. You will be telling me next, it's Merlin's cave we are heading for," she said, smiling. Martin said nothing.

They drove out of the car park in their respective cars, with Martin following Chloe back into Cambridge, and it took nearly half an hour to get there. Once at her home, it only took a relatively short time to load her things into a grip and throw them into Martin's Susuki boot. Martin then aimed his car at North Wales with Chloe Stone by his side.

Chapter Six

Chloe, it turned out, was a bit of a rambler. She surprised Martin when he saw her stuffing clothes, which she thought she might require for a trip up a mountainside into this old, canvas grip. It appeared Chloe only wore her smart apparel as and when she had to, preferring to wear comfy, sloppy jumpers and jeans, which is exactly what she had changed into and was now wearing; Martin also noticed she was not much taller than 1600 mm now that she had taken off her high heels.

As they were travelling back to North Wales, Chloe talked about ancient languages in preconquest times. In fact, she talked most of the way back into North Wales. When they stopped for a coffee and a toilet break and to fill up with fuel, Chloe barely stopped to take a breath. Martin thought she was either excited, nervous, or both. He was grateful for the distraction; all the same, he was aching from all the driving. Chloe continued her tirade and emphasised, as she explained to Martin, how difficult languages were in earlier times, and continued from when Martin had told her when these original documents had been written. "You also have to remember in the 8th century when these works were being penned in," she continued. "The Romans had brought us Latin, which in itself was very difficult for an Englishman and was possibly only used by the more educated people. The Romans left only to be replaced by Angles, the Saxons, and Germanic tribes, not to mention Nordics, all pushing the indigenous people of England further into Wales, Cornwall, Cumbria, and Scotland, which, of course, we now term as Celtics, which still exists in name. Throughout Britain, all these languages were being replaced with a total mixture of what we now term Brittonic or Old English. Add into that mixture, each town and village spoke a particular dialect known and used only by them, and those dialects would be considerably different around the country. On top of that, how do you write something down, and very few people could write anything anyway, something that means the same thing but is pronounced differently when spoken. Consequently, the subjunctive suffix was introduced as it is in the present form; therefore, the intervocalic treatment is better understood."

Martin, who had gone to university, was beginning to think of himself as a bit thick against this extremely knowledgeable person who hardly ever took a breath, but she carried on. "Only the clergy or similar would be able to write anything down anyway, so again, it was down to their interpretation, which almost certainly or most probably contained a religious slant."

Chloe stopped talking, looked at Martin, then

immediately remembered she wasn't lecturing to her students, and at a high university level, she wasn't sure what Martin's background was, so she altered her lecturing status to a more conversational one. "Basically, what was written down by whoever was writing at that time is how they would have said it, but reading it back many years later can be extremely difficult. Especially when you are talking about a language, we know very little about. So, a document written between 1200 and 1300 years ago would have elements of Latin, Old English, and Old French. Add into that mixture a smattering of Greek, possibly even Welsh, and the local dialect on top, and you can start to see the problem of converting it back to a language we understand today."

"So what languages are used in the copies of the documents I have given you, then?" Martin asked, managing to squeeze in a question to the none-stop dialogue that he was only just keeping pace with.

"The papers you have given me that I have looked at so far are mainly Latin. There is a smattering of another vocabulary mixed in there, which has overtones of archaic English and an element that is possibly old French. They probably didn't have transferable words, or the person writing made up a word, as they didn't think anybody else would be reading it, especially 1200 years later. She remained quiet for a second, thinking, then continued. "The Lindisfarne Gospels were written or described as Insular or Hiberno-Saxon art, but they were basically copying the four Gospels, not describing everyday events with ordinary people. And people who couldn't pronounce things properly in what they were trying to convey correctly anyway."

Ignoring the last piece of her dialogue, he said, "That may be a problem," replied Martin. "What I have given you is only a fraction of what there is, and it's been written by the same author over many years. I don't know why he wrote anything, and it could be just the ramblings of or just one man's whim."

Just after 11 o'clock, they eventually arrived back at Martin's house, 8 miles from the Snowden side of Llangollen, in the pitch black, as there is no street lighting. A very cross-black cat, not used to now being left outside all day with only what he could catch to eat and the small amount left for him, shot into the house between Martin and Chloe as they entered through the back door, demanding attention and, more importantly, food. As tired and aching as he was, he scooped out the remainder of his food from a tin already open. "I will have to get a cat flap fitted and leave a tin opener out for you, and then you can help yourself," said Martin, rubbing the top of the cat's head.

"I can see who the boss is with you two," Chloe said, smiling. Between them, they made up the bed in one of the spare bedrooms, making it into something a bit more habitable. Martin had installed an en suite in this room when he had converted the farm, although it had never been used or even tested out. They had a simple supper and went into their separate bedrooms. Martin was absolutely shattered, falling asleep immediately.

The following morning, with a milky sun barely noticeable, they heard each other moving about and greeting each other as they made their way downstairs.

"I've Muesli, which you can add cranberries to. Also, I have eggs and bacon…. and toast if you require something not so healthy."

"Oh! That sounds delicious. I will have that, please, chef. Shall I make some coffee? Is Raffles having the same as yesterday?" asked Chloe. "Or is he invited into the main part of the house? He looks miserable in the utility room."

"I have only just been adopted by him and called him Raffles. I don't even know his surname."

They chatted about the surrounding area whilst breakfast was cooked, Chloe being in charge of the toaster as well as the kettle. They ate every morsel cooked, then did some more toast with marmalade on it. It appeared Chloe didn't have to worry about what she ate to keep her figure. After clearing away and washing up, Martin laid out all the papers he had copied to date. So, equipped with a pencil and paper along with her laptop computer, she gradually pieced together portions of the text.

After two hours of total silence, Chloe sat back with a backache, drinking her third coffee and looking totally mesmerised. "I have done, as you can see, as much as I can. With both my knowledge of languages and odd words from my computer, I have pieced it together as best I can. Of all these pages, two seem to be the cure for ailments and are pretty revolting, too. These two are prophecies. Unfortunately, there is a lot in there I don't understand, but this one," she waved it in the air, "I can only describe it as a sort of diary or part of one, but it isn't, as there are no dates. It has the makings of something ground-shattering, and it needs more work to be spent on it. But from what I can understand so far, the information it contains could well be worth a fortune."

"In what way is it worth anything other than intrinsic value for some very old papers?"

"OK, before I answer that, let me ask you another question: how many sheets of parchment are there? When I say parchments, if it's that old, it would be vellum, a writing material made of very thin skin, which in itself doesn't last, vermin, and other creepy-crawlies like eating it.

"Vermin and other nasties cannot gain access to where it is. The size of the book is about this big," Martin said, holding his arms out to demonstrate how big it was, and then added, "And about 100 to 125 millimetres thick."

"Bede, who wrote about the ecclesiastical history of the English people and is all about Anglo-Saxon living, I think it was finished about 740, roughly the same time frame as yours. Bede's book, which is less than half the size of your parchments, is not just virtually priceless but is priceless. There are very few documents relating to that period that have survived, so at a rough guess, without seeing it, we are talking about possibly many millions."

After a short while, neither of them spoke, Chloe added. "If it's as important as I think it might be, it needs to be in a museum, or at least an institute that can analyse and understand it. Also, it could fill in the gaps in history that we know little about."

Martin looked across the table, then stood up and walked around the room, then sat down again, saying nothing.

"Why is it so important, or, should I say, so difficult for you that you don't want to expose this fantastic find?" she said, trying to understand Martin's dilemma.

Martin again stood up and continued walking around the room, deliberating for many minutes, then sat down again and looked directly into Chloe's eyes. "To be honest, I don't know what to do because once I tell you or show you, it is no longer a secret."

He was still unsure whether to tell this professor everything or nothing, but he continued. "This has possibly been a secret of my family for hundreds of years and of many generations. How many of my past family members knew the existence of these papers, parchments, missives, or whatever you would like to call them, I have absolutely no idea, and I will also add that I was not looking for any of these papers; I came across them completely by accident."

"If I promise never to tell a soul until you give me the OK, but quite honestly, going public would make it safer, as everybody would know about it. Consequently, nobody would try to steal it."

"It's not as simple as that. Do you remember when we left the Red Lion? You laughed at me and thought this was about Merlin? What would you say if I told you I was a direct descendant of Merlin, and before you scoff, I have got absolute proof!"

She was about to laugh, but managed to contain herself, replying. "He was a mythical legend, invented by using stories put about by Geoffrey of Monmouth, wasn't he?"

For an answer, Martin left the room and returned, carrying the old box, and placed it on the table. "When I said it involved my family, this," Martin indicated to the box. "Up until a few days ago, and like the book, I had no idea it existed," he signalled for Chloe to open the box and look at the contents.

Gingerly, she opened the top and peered in, removing the top sheet and reading aloud the last line entered on the Ambrose family tree. "My granddad must have written that regarding the time when my father was born. There is nothing after that. I could fill in my father's and my details, I suppose," Martin took out a handful of papers back to 1593. "This is when our family changed our surname from Ambrosins," another handful of parchments back to 1104. "And this is where Christian names changed slightly," another handful, and the writing was only just legible, but there it was on the last but one page. He carefully placed the sheet in front of Chloe.

She stared at it for some minutes. "This must be one of the best preserved and complete written ancestry family trees in the world." She gently fingered some of the pages, looking at some of the details. After a few minutes, she handed a handful back to Martin to return to the box.

She looked at Martin. "I can see why you were reticent to tell me about this," she said, waving her hand over the contents of the box. For your information, there was a Saint Ambrose who became the bishop of Milan. I think it was in the 4th century. That's where the Ambrosian rite was started. You never know if you could have an ancestor who was a saint. You said a few weeks ago you had no knowledge of any of this, including these?" she said, again waving her hand over the copies of the parchments. "Where did you get these papers and the other parchments from?"

"Never mind my family tree, for the time being, next we must go out, so wrap up warm." They made sandwiches and flasks of coffee, checked for torches, pencils, and paper, putting everything in his rucksack exactly as he had before, then picked up the cat who was on his throne on top of the central heating oil boiler, that always had a nice warm top, especially as Martin had put a thick towel for him to lie on, and looked if he was about to go through the motions of giving himself a wash, and to his disgust put him outside. They then donned the rest of their outdoor clothing and set off for the cave.

After the short drive and parking the car where he had before, he put on the rucksack, and they set off along the lane into the woods and up the mountainside. Chloe never missed a beat; she kept just behind Martin and never stopped talking. Although Martin tried to follow this tirade of words, most were beyond his comprehension. After they had been walking for nearly an hour of strenuous exercise, Martin turned to Chloe and spoke. "See anything interesting?"

Chloe looked around and at the sheer rock in front of her, and suddenly exclaimed. "Steps!"

They walked, or rather scrambled, up the stone steps to the top. Once there, she took in the magnificent views over the Dee valley. "Wow," was her only word. She looked around the small plateau and spoke. "Now, where, more climbing?"

"We are here."

"Can't see any cave," said Chloe, looking around.

"Try tapping the rocks and saying 'open sez-a-me," he smiled, but said it to see if the stone would move for someone or anybody else, so to amuse Martin and herself, she did as he teasingly asked. It didn't take long, as there was little to tap.

"No, I give up. What should happen?"

Martin walked over to the enormous rock against the side of the mountain and, as before, placed his hand on it. As before, it glided back to reveal the opening.

Chloe stepped back in absolute amazement with her mouth open. "That's absolutely incredible." Martin, turned on the torches he had brought with them and entered; Chloe gingerly followed. "Will it close?"

"It hasn't been done yet," came back his reply.

Chloe saw the oversized book as soon as she entered, walked over to it, and stroked it reverently. Martin placed a lamp above the book for her to study it further. She turned the pages and stared at its contents, mesmerised. She looked closer and remained in that position for over an hour, then stood back in a sort of trance. Martin realised that when she was studying, especially something that had interested her, it would be the only time when she was quiet and didn't speak. After a while, she shook her head, trying to gather her composure and restore some semblance of order.

"What else is there?" she asked as she glanced around. "I can see a pestle and mortar, a table in the centre. Oh! Is that another room?" She strode over to it. Martin tried to warn her about what was in there, but the minute she entered the room carrying the light in front of her and above her head, she saw the skeleton, but not batting an eye, she said, "Was that Merlin?"

"I believe so," replied Martin, then he continued.

"This is only a quick look, so you didn't think I was totally loco. We have to go shopping. I have absolutely no food in the house. We can go out to *The Grouse* for a meal tonight, but we must leave now as it will be dark soon. Would you like a sandwich and a coffee before we go back?"

They ate the snack and drank the coffee. Looking over the Dee Valley, she turned to Martin and asked. "I can see why you were reluctant to say anything, but I still feel this book should be deposited into a museum. How safe is it anyway?"

"I will demonstrate shortly," then, without saying a word, he packed the torches, the empty flask, and the snack box back into his rucksack and walked away from the cave, leaving it wide open, with Chloe following him, trying to grapple with leaving a priceless artefact for anybody to steal, and also started down the steps. Halfway down the steps, the massive rock moved back into position with its unmistakable sound. He glanced back at Chloe, who was immediately behind him. "That sound you have just heard is the front of the cave closing. As far as I know, the only person in the world who can move it is me, unless there are any more relatives, but I am sure I am the only living one."

They continued back down the steps and returned to the car, with Chloe absolutely silent. She was obviously in deep thought all the way back to Martin's home. Well, that's one way to keep her quiet for a while, he thought.

Chapter Seven

Before returning to the drive of his house, they continued along the A5 and straight into Llangollen and into the *Aldi* superstore car park. Then, they proceeded to walk up and down the aisles, throwing things in the basket as they went along. They purchased far too much food for the two of them, most of which was bad for anybody, but neither cared. Then, they returned home, storing all the food away in the appropriate places around the kitchen. Martin had brought another 30 tins of cat food and only hoped he liked rabbit and fish, as *Aldi* didn't sell mouse-flavoured, and stored them with the others in one of the cupboards in the utility room.

"I hope he likes *Aldi* food. So far, he has only had food from the local shop, but the cat food there is more than twice the price of *Aldi*."

"Cats are very discerning creatures; they will soon let you know if they don't like it."

They then locked up and jumped back in the car, aiming it first at Lidiart-y-parc, turning left and onto Carrog. She told him to stop when they were halfway across the River Dee, going over the ancient bridge. "Wow, this is some bridge; do you know how old it is?"

"Apparently, there is a stone that the markings indicate was built in 1660. Although difficult to see, I am reliably informed that you can only see it through the moonlight. Whether you believe that or not, it's open for debate. However, we will come back when it's daylight, as it's quite picturesque as well as deathly quiet.

The Grouse was a lively pub and served good, wholesome food. It was quite busy, and they were lucky to get a table. Both had hunter's chicken and spotted dick for dessert, and both talked about their earlier lives.

The following day was rainy and very cold. Well, it was now the beginning of November, and it usually rained in Wales anyway. No matter what month it was, it didn't deter them from returning to the cave. Once there, they spent hours transcribing notes out of Merlin's book, both taking turns and adding a small pencil number at the bottom of each page they copied, putting the same number on the sheets copied as a cross-reference. It was back-breaking work, but they made inroads into the book.

Aching all over as they started their homeward trip, Martin noticed Chloe was now more on the side of leaving the book where it was, at least for the time being. Martin had come to the conclusion that Chloe would be a very good contender for an Olympic medal in talking; thankfully, she at least contained it to material that Martin could understand. They were soaking wet by the time they arrived back at Martin's house. They showered, changed, and went out again to *The Grouse* for another tasty meal. Martin wondered if they would get to eat all the food purchased from *Aldi*. They talked about Merlin's cave and speculated on what they may discover written amongst all the copied pages and the mountain of those yet still to be copied.

The following day, Martin returned Chloe to Cambridge, along with some of the food they had yet to eat, complete with all the papers they had meticulously copied down from the book, which Martin also had photocopied for his records. Chloe had wanted to take the book back to Cambridge with her, but Martin was very much against it, and as he reminded her, "If it's worth what you think it is, it's far safer where it is, apart from anything else, I doubt if I would be able to carry it down those steps."

On the return journey to Cambridge, Chloe asked Martin where he had spent his childhood. "Rutland," was his immediate reply, and he thought he ought to put a bit of meat on the bone rather than just the one-word answer. "A little village called Exton, a stone's throw from where Rutland water is now. The property is at the edge of a wood just outside the village, actually."

"You said that both your parents are dead. You also told me you had Pickfords to clear the house contents and put them into storage. How many of your family members lived in your old house? What happened to the house? The reason I asked is that I was just wondering if there were any indications left there pertaining to your family's past. They may reveal something about Merlin."

"The house was between 150 and 200 years old, possibly a bit older; I think it is part of a big estate belonging to the Duke of Rutland."

Martin then went quiet for a bit before continuing. "Do you know, I always assumed the house belonged to the Duke's estate? My grandparents lived there, and my father and I lived there in my younger years. Other than that, I have absolutely no idea if the Duke owns it or not. My father never sold it, that was for sure, and I have done nothing with it. It would be easy enough to find out."

They eventually reached Chloe's flat in Cambridge, and after a cup of tea and a few custard creams, Martin started back to North Wales. Many hours later, when he arrived back, he was totally shattered. He had got fish and chips again in Llangollen on the way through and had them with a cup of tea back at his house. As he never ate all the fish, he gave what was left to Raffles. But he was wondering what on earth he was going to do with all the remaining food he had purchased while Chloe was here, so before retiring to bed, he threw most of it into the freezer.

Early in the morning, he looked at some of the notes written on the papers left behind that Chloe had made earlier. Although they were incomplete, she had written basically what they were about on the top of each sheet. The Welsh uprising is what Chloe had put on one, and on another, in the middle hundred. On others, there was writing, but he understood them even less. She had taken many sheets back with her to Cambridge and left Martin feeling a little uncomfortable about that, but he believed she was an honest person and could be trusted; he certainly had to trust somebody if he was to find out anything about what Merlin had written.

After Martin had left Chloe's flat to return to North Wales, Chloe lay out all the pages from the book, which they had both meticulously copied down, and she set about excitedly deciphering. There were many words she knew she wouldn't be able to translate. Others would need further investigations. Even so, she thought that some words would be lost totally in their translation.

She worked for many hours on each page over the following week at her home in Cambridge. Some of the pages were for ailments and listed revolting cures, which, once she realised what they were, she put to one side. Others, though, were far more interesting subjects; one page she thought was of extreme importance. But there were probably two-thirds of the book back in the cave, still untouched. Each time she left her flat to go shopping or to work, she gathered all the papers up together and stored them safely away.

It was on a Saturday, 10 days after visiting North Wales, while she was totally engrossed and in the middle of deciphering a very interesting piece, following some words, she noticed the *Ismere Diploma,* which is a document known from that period. It appeared that Merlin must have written at least part of that particular piece of material by order of Bretwalda Aethelbald, which basically meant the king, Bretwalda, or English ruler. According to Merlin, a man named Cuthred tried to kill him for knowing too much after writing, or part of writing, the *diploma*. Culthred had a motto: *'Keep a secret. Tell nobody or leave nobody to tell.'*

Just then, her phone rang, making her jump. Chloe picked it up, cross to be disturbed. It was her mother's neighbour who conveyed the information that her mum had been rushed off to the hospital. Chloe grabbed her handbag and a few things and shot off to Cambridge General Hospital at top speed, or at least as fast as the traffic would allow her to go.

She arrived 40 minutes later, having struggled to find a parking spot. The hospital was ghostly quiet at this time of night, but thankfully, the reception desk was still manned or womaned, as it was a young lady behind the counter. She explained that she had just received a call that her mother had been brought in. The receptionist told Chloe which ward her mother was in, then ended up running down what seemed like miles of corridors to reach the ward where her mother was ensconced.

She approached the ward sister, who, according to her name tag, was Jayden Bell. She asked how Mrs. Stone was, reiterating to her that she was her daughter. "Your mum broke her leg falling downstairs. They took her to the orthopaedic after having it x-rayed. Unfortunately, when she arrived there, she had a heart attack, so they immediately returned her here. We are monitoring her, but she is in a lot of pain. They will be taking her back into the theatre shortly, I believe."

Chloe went to see her mum lying in a bed with a sheet tucked under her chin. She hardly recognised her for a start; she looked so small and was surrounded by tubes and wires. Chloe sat on the chair next to the bed holding her mum's hand, telling her mum everything that she had been discovering over her research into Merlin's papers, for no other reason but to distract from her obvious discomfort, although whether she knew Chloe was even there or not, she had no way of telling, Chloe hadn't been there for more than 20 minutes when a porter came and took her mum back into theatre.

It was two hours later when a tired-looking, very sombre surgeon came and told Chloe that her mother had died on the theatre table following complications after another heart attack, and how very sorry he was for her loss. So, with a very sad and desperate feeling, she walked out of the hospital and back into the night rain.

She walked around the city, getting wetter by the minute. Eventually, she sat under the shelter near Trinity College, deciding to ring Martin on her mobile while looking at her watch. She nearly shut it off when she realised the time, but Martin answered the call. "Hello," he said in a somewhat sleepy voice.

She poured out everything that had happened to her mother, so when she had finished her tale, he said it in his lovely, calm voice. "Go back to your home, pack a bag, and come over to Wales. You would be more than welcome. At least it will take your mind off losing your mum."

"I think I would like that, but I have no idea what time I will get there."

She retrieved her car once she remembered where she had parked it and went back to her apartment, which was on the outskirts of Cambridge; it was probably a separate village at one time, as the area was still called Arbury.

She had been away for well over four hours and had left in a hurry to get to the hospital, but as soon as she got to her front door, she found it open, 'I wouldn't have left my front door open,' she thought and entered with trepidation, once inside her eyes fell immediately on the table she had been working on, where Martin's many papers that had been and brought from Wales, but not one was there now. She phoned the police immediately. "I am terribly sorry, madam, there is no way anybody would be able to visit at this time of night, err, or should I say this morning. I can promise you somebody will ring tomorrow sometime. Unfortunately, theft is not a high priority these days."

She then went on to explain that what had been stolen was priceless information. Also, according to her, they had been stolen while she was tending to her mother in the hospital. She added, "She has just passed away."

With a pacified sigh, whether or not the person on the other end of the phone felt sorry for her, she didn't know. "I will try my best to get somebody to call you back shortly," and rang off.

Chapter Eight

When Martin had returned to North Wales after taking Chloe back to Cambridge some ten days earlier, he had been thinking about those conversations he had had with her about his earlier life. Times back in Rutland, when his father was alive and they both were living in this property, he always assumed it belonged to the Duke of Rutland's estate. The estate owned most of the land and buildings all around there, or at least used to. He decided to look through all the paperwork that he had retrieved from the tea chests. Some of the papers were still in the barn, remembering that some had looked like legal documents, as well as other related solicitors' paraphernalia, these he had stored separately in his back bedroom from the time he was looking for family information, and before he found the box with the family tree inside, then remembered seeing some solicitors' letters.

So at 9 o'clock the following morning, with breakfast cleared away and coffee in hand, he started looking through the piles of papers collected from both the tea chest in the barn and what he had retained from the other tea chests beforehand, which were now all piled up together on the kitchen table. Placing his cup down, he lifted the first few papers out of the box, including guarantees and invoices for all manner of things. He placed them all into a black bin liner. There were letters to Martin's father when he went to scout camp, now in the bin liner, operating instruction manuals and materials for a carport 30 years previously, as well as the purchase of a car well over 30 years ago. The search went on; papers jumbled up in no particular order.

After a further coffee and about halfway down the tea chest, he came across solicitor's letters for services rendered dated 1923. He placed them to one side, and a few more pages down came a plan for the house in Rutland, dated 1923. The house was called Tunneley Wood; this had been a very big wood at one time, and the house was built inside it. Now, as far as Martin could recall, the only wood left was that inside the 25 acres which went with the house. He placed that with the solicitor's letter. He came across army records belonging to his grandfather, who was a sergeant in the Royal Artillery in the last war. He decided to save those; next was another solicitors letter dated 1920 regarding a search referring to a railway link between LMS and GWR, and another letter from the same solicitors, but this time in 1934 regarding a military air force base, Martin knew Cottesmore Airbase was only down the road; they could have been searching the area for the best place to build it, but surely he mused, they wouldn't have contacted the Ambrose's unless they owned the property. Maybe his family had owned the property after all. He then put the entire solicitor's correspondence together, along with the letters he had found beforehand. Then, hoping the solicitors were still in business, the only way of finding that out was going online, and if they were still about obtaining their telephone number, he thought a three-digit number which was on the letters wouldn't be relevant today, the company was still in business, and Martin rang their telephone number which was a bit longer, starting with 01572.

Martin told them he maybe the owner and the reason why he was, of a house called Tunneley Wood. He gave them his full name and address, where he was now living, and the full address of the property.

"Any information you can give me, I would be extremely grateful," he said, leaving them his phone number in the hope of them returning his call, which is what they told him they would do.

It was an hour later and far sooner than Martin thought possible when the solicitor phoned Martin back and asked him some security questions, such as the name of his father, which made Martin smile as he answered. When they asked him his grandfather's name, he answered. "The same as mine, as were my last 10 generation grandfathers, not very imaginative with new names, my family," he smiled.

Martin could sense the solicitor would have had to

smile. "If you bring in three forms of identity, they will give him the deeds of the property, and its 25 acres. We have always held them for your father. In actual fact, this practice has always carried out your family's actions for many a year. I am sorry to hear your father has passed away," and rang off. Only a solicitor could say such things with a 30-year gap.

He sifted through the rest of the papers and put all the solicitors' letters and correspondence together in a pouch, along with the council tax and water bills.

It was just after 7 o'clock the following morning when Martin set off for his old home in Rutland. It was 143 miles and, according to his satnav, 2 hours and 43 minutes via M6. If he took the alternative A50 route, it was 2 hours and 50 minutes, but only 120 miles; it was the latter route he took. He needed to go to Oakham first, where the solicitors' offices were. He pulled up outside their offices at 10-20, so much for the times on the satnav; mind you, he had stopped for a coffee. Thirty minutes later, he walked out of the solicitor's, got back into his car, and looked through all the paperwork he had been handed while still in the solicitor's car park. He was definitely the owner of the property; he wondered if it was still standing. Well, he thought, there is only one way of finding out.

He drove out of their car park and headed towards Exton via the A606, turned left onto Barnsdale Road, then passed by the late Geoff Hamilton's gardens and onto Exton village. At the far end of Exton, just outside the village, he pulled up outside the large steel gates, which were his former home, and was surprised to see them in one piece. He got out of his car and looked at the gates held together by a large chain and padlock. He remembered putting the chain on, but had no idea where he had put the key. The hedges on each side of the gates were a thick mess and 20 feet high with brambles, buckthorn, and every sharp-needled type of foliage imaginable.

So, where or how was he to enter? Leaving the car where it was, he followed the road and hedge for some time till he came across a large gap, enough to get a car through. In fact, it looked like a vehicle had been through there. He followed the track and came to the old house. It was still standing, which was something. The windows were non-existent, and neither were the doors. Part of the roof had fallen in, and the inside was no better. All the fireplaces had been ripped out, as had anything and everything that was either worth money or burnable. It was sad to see such a mess. The wildlife outside was having a field day. Martin decided to walk the perimeter. It was hard going at first, but then he noticed someone had been tending the area where there were brambles nearer the house. This was worn-down grass. Then he came across a new house that had been built and butted up to where his boundary was, well, what should have been the boundary. It looked as if they had taken over quite a large section of the garden, including three trees, one of which he remembered climbing as a child. He was looking over the ground directly at this new building when a woman came out of the house, demanding what the hell he was doing in **their** wood. Martin was a little taken aback and said in a steely, steady voice, "This is not your wood, madam; I want you to reinstate the boundary to where it should be. You will be hearing from my solicitors at the earliest. Good-bye."

He returned to the house, thinking that if she had adopted a more pleasant attitude, he might well have sold her the piece of land. He dismissed her from his thoughts and entered the house. He was wondering if someone wanted to hide some memorabilia, where they would hide it, assuming they had something to hide in the first place, but the more Martin thought about his family secrets, the more there was to uncover. They all, or at least some of his family, must have known about their past history. Surely, it wouldn't be left to chance for a person like me to stumble across a cave in North Wales halfway up a mountainside. *Surely, no....* the more he thought about it, the more certain he became that there must be more.

The house itself was depressing. Half the ceilings were hanging down, 50% of the plaster was off the walls, and many of the quarry tiles on the floor were missing or somehow were being pushed up. So where? If it were buried outside, it would need a JCB to find it. If indeed there was anything to find, this was hopeless. Another thought just struck him: somebody else could have found whatever it was. Martin continued to wander about the house, with his hands deep inside his pockets, trying to remember where all the furniture had fitted. He was standing in the doorway of what was the kitchen when he heard somebody shouting to gain his attention. He crossed the hallway to be confronted by a large, overbearing man in an expensive-looking suit. "What were you saying to my wife about this being your land?"

Martin looked the man directly in his eyes and, in that disarming quiet voice, replied. "Because it is, and if you want to know, my family has owned it for over 100 years and lived in it for probably twice that long."

"It belongs to the Duke of Rutland, who I happen to be friends with and whom I regularly shoot with, so clear off out of here," he shouted.

"Who you shoot with is no concern of mine. What is of concern to me is that you immediately remove what you think is yours and return to the original boundary. I haven't yet checked, but if you have built on any of my land, and it looks very much like it, get your builders to remove it. You will receive a letter from my solicitor shortly. Good day to you."

Martin was just turning back into the house when the man realised he was in the wrong. "Look, I can't alter that garden. We would have none left, and my kids would be devastated. It's the main part. As far as I know, you haven't bothered with this house for years. Could we come to some agreement?"

"Speak to my solicitor when you receive their letter. I will not deal with you out here, especially when you try bullying and shouting to get your own way. It doesn't wash with me. Now, would you please get off my land?" the man stuttered and stammered, turning and walking off.

Once the man was gone, Martin took out his mobile and rang the solicitors and told them what had taken place, "Could you look up the property and their planning application, get somebody to do some measuring if it's needed, put the wind-up to the people who have built that house. I don't mind selling them the land, so come up with a figure and make sure your bill is included. Thank you very much."

Going back into the house, he stood in the hallway again, thinking, 'If I wanted to hide something like a box, for instance, where would I hide it? Why would anybody want to?' But the nagging at the back of his mind kept telling him, there would be something, and quite possibly important, but what?'

He sat on the bottom step of the stairs where he used to sit as a small child, trying to think of anything that may have occurred when he was that child. He peered around the large hall and then used the newel post to lift himself up. It was the only piece left of the banisters, so he swung around and looked under the stairs. Some of the quarry tiles had been dislodged even under there, 'now there's a place not easily disturbed,' he thought. He knelt down and removed some more of the tiles, then some more, and pulled the soft sand-like material that is always beneath this type of flooring away. He had moved the best part of a metre when his fingertips felt something hard but had a covering. It was quite difficult to get to; it was directly under the bottom step. By more and more diligent pawing of the sand, he gradually managed to remove a substantial amount.

A few moments later, he managed to retrieve a small box wrapped in an oilskin cloth. He placed it on the bottom step of the stairs to have a closer look after removing the now very damaged oilskin to reveal what looked like an oak box. It was about 160 mm square and about 85-90 mm deep, having what looked like a small lock. He knew that he had the key at home to fit that lock, one of the keys found in the box of his ancestry tree. He came for something that was possibly hidden that his family must have known about, and he had done that. So, after a quick last look around his childhood home for the final time, he retraced his way back to his car, placed the box in the boot, and set off back to Wales.

While travelling along the M54 motorway, he realised he had had very little to eat and was getting very hungry. Although he would never normally eat in a motorway café, this stretch of motorway was devoid of any such luxury. He continued on as it changed to an 'A' class road, the A5, and was able to turn off and head towards a small village called Atcham. This village had a good restaurant called the Mytton and Mermaid, and it was directly opposite the gates of a National Trust property called Attingham Park.

It was getting late when Martin arrived very tired back in North Wales, but he was also excited and apprehensive about what was in the small box. He retrieved the two keys he had found in the ancestry box where he had left them, then examined the wooden box he had found under the stairs. It had been beautifully made, with the exception of one corner. It was still in perfect condition, made of oak, and very smooth, considering how old it looked. Although it was old, it certainly was not ancient. He inserted the correct key. It turned smoothly with very little pressure. Inside the wooden box, which was lined with white silk, was a much smaller box. This box was exquisite, unbelievably ornate, and quite heavy, and by its look, it was made out of solid gold. He couldn't see any assay marks anywhere around the outside. He selected the other key, if that's what you could call it. It was a key like no other he had ever seen, very small, the head had a sort of Celtic design, the barrel part was round with another smaller round piece inside the barrel, and he wasn't sure how it worked. There was nothing to indicate how or even if the key turned. He slotted the key into the small round hole that had obviously been designed for it, but nothing happened. He turned it, but nothing happened. He pushed it further in, and there was a small click. He opened the box not by a hinge but by lifting the top off. It was so well made that the actual lid was inside the top.

'Exquisite' was not a good enough word for the workmanship that went into making this box. He removed a small parchment with minuscule writing on it, as well as what looked like two small pieces of carved bone, or ivory, from inside a small kid leather pouch. This was a mystery. Was this beautiful box worth preserving for these things, which looked like nothing more than insignificant items? He then wondered how old the items were. Were they the same age as the book in Merlin's cave? He took a very careful photo of the parchment, which had been folded over twice. Once flattened out, it was still only about A5-sized paper. He would enlarge the writings later before he replaced everything back as he had found it. He got hold of a magnifying glass and inspected the two pieces of carved bone. They looked like some Celtic designs had been etched onto them.

Tomorrow, he would deposit it into the bank vault for safekeeping, but there was definitely a secret there. What it was, however, was indeed a mystery in itself.

Chapter Nine

Police Sergeant Roy Greisley was working nights all this week; he was based at Parkside Police Station in Cambridge. He was also a lay preacher at the local Methodist church in Milton, where he lived with his wife and two small children. As a policeman in a fairly low crime rate area, he normally dealt with the odd drunk and minor driving offences. Rarely anything juicy happened, so when a call came in from the central office informing him that a young lady had just had a break-in whilst visiting her mother, who had just passed away in the hospital, he decided to ring her. "Can you tell me what has been stolen?" he asked her in his most placatory way.

"Priceless information. I had been translating the scripts, which are on loan," came back with the reply, and then added, "I am a professor at the University. The papers that were stolen are thankfully only copies of some very old documents; the originals are extremely old and would be quite valuable, and they don't belong to me."

The police sergeant gave the standard reply. "Somebody may contact you in the morning." She became very distressed, telling the sergeant how upset she was just after losing her mum, so after some deliberation, he agreed to go and see her at her home.

A Short time later, the police sergeant, accompanied by a constable, arrived at Chloe's house on Holland Street. Knowing there would be little, if anything, they could do to help her, especially at this time of night, they knocked on her door. She invited them in and reiterated what she had previously told the sergeant over the phone about the papers. "The papers were worthless in themselves, she had said, but they had been copied directly from an extremely poignant source. I brought them back here to translate them into understandable English. What I was gradually learning in doing so was both revealing and disturbing. Those few pages, gentlemen, would change certain aspects of what we know about Anglo-Saxon life and are basically priceless. Also, if they end up in the wrong hands, they could be completely misconstrued, to say the very least."

The two policemen took notes of all these unusual particulars. "If these papers are not the originals, where are the originals kept then?"

"I cannot tell you that," she replied.

"Can you tell us, then, what was written on them?"

"I would prefer not to tell you that either."

"What sort of language are they written in if you were making them into understandable English?"

"I would prefer to decline to tell you that also."

"So let me get this straight," said the sergeant. "You

have acquired, sorry, have been loaned these papers, but you don't want to tell me where they are from or by whom they belong. Also, you say what is written on them is priceless, but you can't tell me what it is. You have translated most of the papers you have, but have no intention of telling me what is actually written down on them?"

"That just about sums it up."

"It doesn't leave us much to go on, though," and then added. "Are there more of the same?"

"I don't think I should tell you that either."

"Who knew about the papers?"

"The man who owns them obviously…. and has paid me to translate them. I rang him at his home in North Wales a few minutes ago. The only other person I have told is the Dean of Trinity College. I had to ask him for time off to study the papers because they are extremely important."

"You had better give us the address of the Dean so we can go and question him." She went off to get her address book and told them, which they wrote down in their small black notebook, and with that, they left.

On the way down the stairs from Chloe's second-floor flat, the young police constable made a grab at a piece of paper. It was a single sheet of ordinary A4 copy paper, which was tight up against a wheelie bin. He stared at the contents. "Serge, I think this is one of her papers that the professor was telling us about. The thief must have dropped it when he left.”

“Bring it with you into the car, and we’ll have a look at what all the fuss is about,” said the sergeant. Once they were both seated, they stared at the neat handwriting under each piece of what could only be described as gobbledegook to the two policemen.

After a short while, the constable was the first to speak. “According to this translation, earthworks were built and completed in 768 by Polytheism under Corvee, bracketed ‘labour’ by the orders of Bishops. To shut all non-Christians into Cymry, bracketed ‘Wales’, which took 50 years to complete,” said the young constable.

“They may be referring to Offa’s dyke. I thought Offa had it built only to segregate Wales from England and had nothing to do with religion, let alone segregating Christians from non-believers,” came the reply from the Sergeant. “Get your smartphone out. When was the dyke built?”

The constable fiddled with his smartphone for a few moments, then read out. “Started in 785.”

“I don’t know who wrote this garbage, then, but something doesn't add up. If Offa started the dyke in 785, and this says it was finished in 768 and took 30 years to build, Offa had nothing to do with it. They certainly had no JCBs to help them. Look up Polytheism and Corvée, will you? I am not even sure what they mean.”

“Hang on,” said the constable as he tapped away on the keys. “Corvée means unpaid labour. Polytheism, they worship in the belief of Deities, that's double-dutch to me."

"But not to me," said his sergeant, suddenly thinking hard. "What this paper is claiming is that non-Christian people, pagans to you and me, were forced into building that dyke by Christian Bishops, and they dug it 70-odd years before Offa was the king of England, or whatever he was?"

"I don't see that as so terrible. Surely, most wars seem to be caused by religion. Building a ditch for what you believe in sounds like a better proposition, better than killing entire sections of society, and didn't pagans have ritual killings? Sounds like a bit of their own medicine to me. Are pagans the same as these Poly-watsits? Worshipping deities sounds more like drawing a handkerchief out of their pocket rather than drawing a sword out of a scabbard. Anyway, she did say it was shattering information and wasn't prepared to tell us what was written."

The sergeant started the car and aimed it towards the Dean's house. "Christianity has been around for two thousand years," he said as he pulled in behind a van going past. "In that time and within that time scale, no one has questioned anything with regard to the transformation from heathens and pagans into law-abiding citizens because Christianity is correct. Also, I believe in it. It's all about loving they neighbour, turning the other cheek, doing unto others, etc., and on the whole, that is why civilisation works. This one sheet is damning enough. There are probably many more of these papers, according to Professor Stone. I don't think a man of the cloth, such as a Bishop, would order people into a certain area, such as Wales, just because they were not sure of Christianity. They would have converted them. Anyway, who was supposed to have written this garbage?"

At that minute, they pulled up outside the address given to them. It was now in the early hours of the morning when the two policemen got out of the car and knocked on the door. And it was a large old stone building; the front of the house was next to the road. They waited and knocked harder. First, the lights came on, and then a woman's voice asked who it was. Once established who they were, the door opened. "Is the Dean in?" asked the sergeant.

"Yes, fast asleep in bed, why?"

"We are sorry to disturb you, madam, but we would like a quick word with him. It is quite important."

She disappeared upstairs and re-emerged with the Dean, who was doing up his dressing gown and following her downstairs. "What is this all about? Could it not wait till morning?" he asked crossly, if not a little pompously.

"Sorry for the inconvenience, sir. Could I ask you what your movements have been this evening?"

"Returned home after a meeting at Trinity at about 8 o'clock and have been here all night with my wife."

"Am I right in that Ms Chloe Stone asked you if she could have time off to study some ancient documents?" asked the sergeant, getting out his notebook and pen.

"Yes," replied the Dean.

"Did you tell anybody else about that?"

"Yes, I did, two people, in fact, Stanley Gibson, the bursar, and Richard Watkins, the treasurer, both from Trinity College."

"Did Ms. Stone ask you not to tell anybody, at least until she had completed some of the research she was doing? According to Ms Stone, she told you that the gentleman who owns the originals of these papers was reticent about letting them out of his safekeeping and did so by expressing that, as far as security is concerned, nobody else was to be told?"

"Well, yes, she did. As a matter of fact, these people are not just anybody, though, but important people for the smooth running of the college. What is all this about? I am getting cold."

"Could you please give me the addresses of both those gentlemen?" The Dean disappeared back into the house for his address book, and the sergeant wrote them down as the Dean recited them. "For your information, sir, Ms. Stone's house was broken into, and the papers she was working on have all been stolen."

"Before you try to disturb either of these gentlemen, I can tell you now that Richard Watkins has been on holiday since the weekend, on a cruise, actually, and isn't due back till next weekend. And would you please use her correct title? It is Professor Stone, not Ms. Goodnight," closing the door, a bit too hard.

It was barely 30 minutes later when they drove to the bursar's house. Mr Gibson had a large house in the village of Fulbourn, with a large curved drive to the front. As they pulled up, security lights came on, illuminating the entire front. The two police officers again banged on the front door of his house. A minute passed, the lights came on inside, and then a very annoyed man opened the door, demanding what they wanted.

"I want to know of your movements tonight, sir?" the sergeant asked in just as terse a manner.

"I'm sure it could wait till morning," he answered superciliously. "But if you must know, I came home about 6 o'clock and have been here all night."

"Can anybody corroborate that statement, sir?"

"No, I live by myself," looking more than a little flustered.

At that minute, the constable appeared in the doorway and asked, "If you have been home since 6 o'clock, can I ask you why your car bonnet is still warm?" Then he added. "Do you always go to bed fully clothed, sir?"

"Err, I, I, I, went for some wine, it's the other side of town," he stammered.

"What time would that be, sir?"

"Er, not sure about 10 o'clock, and why are you

asking me these silly questions? I am sure it will wait till morning.”

“The people in the wine shop will be able to corroborate your story, will they, as well as confirm those items you purchased, do you think?” asked the sergeant, ignoring his last demand.

“I have no idea. Now, if you have finished, I will go back to bed,” and with that, he slammed the door.

As the two police officers drove away, they both knew that Gibson was lying, and as Richard Watkins was away on holiday with his wife, it would be pointless even thinking he had anything to do with the robbery, which left Gibson not only the only suspect but the most likely.

Chapter Ten

It wasn't until coming up to 3 o'clock in the morning, when Chloe, being very cold and upset, as well as disappointed, that she set about driving to Martin's house in North Wales. She had promised she would look after all the papers that she had been entrusted with, but she had let him down. With packed bags, she got into her car, set her satnav with Martin's postcode in, and set off.

She had no idea anybody would be following her, but became a little concerned when she pulled into Corley services some two hours later on the M6. She was easily able to park just outside the main entrance of the establishment at this time in the morning, which was just as well, the weather had turned colder and had now started to rain, but she was still surprised by how much traffic there was about as she went in to have a coffee, just to keep herself awake as much as anything. Before continuing her journey, she filled the car with fuel, which she thought was far more expensive than back home. As she pulled away, she had a strange feeling she was being followed, but was arguing with herself why anybody would. That niggling feeling was still there, but it wasn't until she was going around all the traffic islands that were on the A5, which were either near or around Oswestry. She was becoming uncomfortable, then certain she was being followed, especially after going past the Chirk roundabout. Chloe, along with those same headlights behind her, was the only vehicle on the road, but she was too tired to think of what to do. At 7:30, she pulled up outside Martin's farmhouse, hoping no police were about to clock her speeding. Martin helped her into the house, putting her straight to bed in the same room as before.

It was early afternoon when Chloe came downstairs fully dressed and very hungry. The amount of food Chole could put away, she should be 20 stone, not this slim, elegant creature she was. Martin had made a lamb stew with dumplings, which he served up with aplomb. "Would madam partake in a glass of dry chardonnay?" he said, appearing behind her with a wine bottle in hand and a tea towel draped over his arm.

She smiled for the first time since leaving her house. "Thank you, kind sir." While they ate their dinner, Chloe told Martin everything that had happened, and when she finished, she said, "The funny thing is, I could swear I was being followed. I had one car behind me all the way, especially more noticeable after leaving the motorway, as there was so little traffic it was quite apparent."

"We will have to be very vigilant from now on in that case. By the way, I bought myself an off-road four-track, much to the amazement of my neighbour, with whom I have been getting on famously. He often pops in for coffee, and I go there for cakes. A great cook is Mrs Griffiths. We came to an agreement about the water that I have, and he wants, some land that I have no use for, which he could use, swapped for lamb he has an abundance of, and I like. He asked me the other day what was so fascinating about the mountains I keep going up to, so I gave him a picture I had painted, so he's chuffed to bits and had it framed. But that is me and my boring life. What I really want to know about is how you got on with those papers. I photocopied them all before you returned to Cambridge, so everything was not lost."

"Some of Merlin's missives, which are totally haphazard and jumbled up, even after I followed our numbering system, and because there is no index or anything related to what he was writing about, or even what year he wrote them, it's difficult to put it into context or any sort of order; the only thing I kept telling myself is, that no matter how farfetched we think the writings are today, they would have been factual when he wrote them. Also, that is how Merlin saw or believed when writing about all these things at the time. There are some pages regarding potions, mainly to relieve bodily problems, which could be anything from warts to relieving pain after losing a limb. Some of his concoctions are pretty horrific. Apparently, once a potion was made up, it would be left out to ferment or finish off by the sun or, in some cases, the moon. There is no mention of whether they worked or not, but what it does indicate is Merlin was a Druid, or what we now think of as a Druid, using plants and planets to guide him." Can I use your phone? I must ring up an undertaker and get my mother's funeral organised."

Martin thought she was quite incredible, how she could change the subject completely in the middle of a conversation. "Tell you what, I will sort out the undertaker and ring him up for you; have you got a death certificate yet?"

"No, but the doctor said he would leave it with the ward sister later today."

"You may need that before they agree to do anything. Let's see what happens when I have a word with them."

"Some other pages we had copied were extremely interesting," she carried on as if she hadn't thought of or said anything else. "One referred to an agreement called the *'ismere diploma,'* which we know is a document drawn up in 736. It refers to a donation of 10 hides to Husmerae in an area called Ismere."

Martin interjected. "What is, or how big is, an area of 10 hides? Who is Husmerae, and where is Ismere?"

"I will tell you what the facts are first, and then what is actually known about the *ismere diploma.* The document is written in Latin. It has been written by more than one hand and is in the British Museum, where this book of Merlin's should be. I am positive that the document must have been partly written by Merlin; the hand is identical, but I only know that as I am the only person to have seen **both** documents. On the back of the document is where King Aethelbald of Mercia grants 10 hides to *Cyneberht,* for a minster, 'which may or may not be a Cathedral by the way'. Husmerae were a tribe or clan of people based in the Midlands. The piece of land called Ismere has been debated for years and is thought to straddle the river Stour, which includes a very large forest. That part is easy to understand as the signatures for the diploma are on the front, and the grant of 10 hides is on the rear of the said document. I don't think that in those days, signatures had to be at the bottom of a document, and one of those signatures was of a man named *Cuthred.* All that is well documented, but nobody has understood what the Diploma actually meant till now. The next part of this narrative is now what I found out from some of Merlin's papers: the king had given this land away, but it wasn't the King's to give. It was *Cuthred's,* and it was not to build a minster, but a place called a minster. Now, I looked up an ordinance map of the area in question, and lo and behold, there is a place which has since changed its name to Kidderminster. The Husmerae tribe joined forces with Wiogorna, who were prouvincia, an administrative division of which this Cyneberht was one, which would then make the area into a sub-kingdom. Now, at this time, land and power were everything. This begs the question, why would the kingdom of Mercia want or need a sub-kingdom in the centre of its own? Well, Merlin knew why. The answer is somewhere in his book. However, I mentioned *Cuthred;* I think he was instrumental to everything at that time. We know for a fact he raided Wales on numerous occasions. Now, Merlin almost certainly lived for some time in South Wales and would have been classed as a scholar. Don't forget that the only people literate at that time were those in monastic Circles. However, not everybody trusted monks. On one page of this book, Merlin states he moved to England and presumably moved on to the cave where he died. Unfortunately, we have no dates. One man on a mule could travel anywhere without raising a hair, and I feel that *Cuthred* wanted Merlin dead. He had almost certainly already killed *Aethelbald."*

"Flipping heck, is it all as complex as that?" said Martin, exhausted from trying to take in all that information.

"Well, you have to remember, for years, people have been guessing at what you have uncovered as in this book, so you have to disseminate fact from fiction even though we have been indoctrinated towards what we now know is the fiction, probably because at that time it was either easier for the masses to understand or the church altered it for their own reason.

The next thing I came across was this. Have you ever heard the word *corvée?"*

"No."

"Well, the word is old French with a root from Latin.

It means unpaid labour, not to be mixed up with slavery. Cathedrals were mainly built under corvée rule, inasmuch as 'if you want it, then you build it,' Or, if you don't build it, then you won't go to heaven, which would be a kind of blackmail."

"There was I, thinking the only thing of any use in the scribbling of this old book would be absolute tosh."

"Well, no, and far from it, what else did I find out, with the limited amount of information to hand with regards to the book? Offa's dyke, we have all been led to believe, was built by King Offa, so hence the title, and it was thought it was simply to divide England from Wales, but nobody has come up with the reason why anybody would want to do this. Well, according to Merlin, it was built by what he says were *polytheistic* people, as you are probably aware. They worshipped deities, and before you ask, they were around a thousand years before Christianity."

"I thought pagans were before Christians?"

"Well, yes and no, nothing about Paganism was actually written down. However, we know about polytheism as it was all over the continent, especially in Rome, where people were educated and could write about everything that was going on. We only assume things about Pagans. I personally think they have had a bad press; there is no absolute proof of mass sacrifices or even sacrificial killings, and they may have been a very caring group of people."

"What about Druids, then?"

"Again, all we genuinely know about Druids is as much as we know about Pagans, and we guess or claim they worshipped the cycles of nature, which they may or may not have done. For years, we said, or were told, that they built Stonehenge, but that alone has now been dismissed as an impossibility. I have been told those stones came from South Wales, and the Seven Estuary separates them. I am hoping Merlin may enlighten us about who built it and the reason why, but it was built possibly two to three thousand years before Merlin. Anyway, we are getting off the subject, going back to Offa's dyke. According to Merlin and who must have been around at that time, it was Bishops, and remember, in those days Bishops were not necessarily religious people, well it was those people who ordered for the dykes to be built, or better to describe their actions as 'dug', by all who were not prepared to worship Christianity, which would have included Polytheism, Pagans, Druids and even heathens, Can I have another cup of coffee, its rather nice, but according to Merlin's writings," she continued again in mid-sentence. A Butterfly mind had nothing on Chloe. Martin went and replenished both their cups with coffee. "He only had one word for all people who didn't classify themselves as the religious group of people called Christians, so he called them all Polytheists. He probably didn't know another word for non-Christians. I am not sure the name Druid or Pagan even existed at that time, certainly not by name. But it's the dates that are fascinating," Chloe continued after taking a mouthful of fresh coffee and asking Martin what type of coffee it was, as she thought she would get some. "These earthworks, which we have been calling Offa's dyke, we are led to believe were finished in about 790 AD and took 15 years to build. But according to what Merlin has written, they took 30 years to build and were started around 738, so Offa couldn't have had anything to do with implementing them other than possibly maintaining them. All those people who didn't or wouldn't practice Christianity were then thrown into Wales from England. Whether the dyke was patrolled or not, I have no idea, and Merlin doesn't say."

"No wonder David was made into a saint with all the heathens of Britain crowding into Wales," added Martin flippantly.

"Hardly, he died at least 100 years earlier as did Saint Winifred, who was another Welsh saint."

Chapter Eleven

It was past 3 o'clock when Martin said, "Time for some more food shopping. I didn't get much in, as I hadn't a clue what sort of food you liked; the last time we went, we just threw anything in the basket. I don't particularly like spiced food."

"Neither do I," was the quick reply. "Personally, I prefer fish and plain types of food." So putting on warm outdoor clothes, started to make their way back to *Aldi* in Llangollen, the picturesque eight-mile journey is delightful and changes dramatically with the seasons, after a slightly better appraisal of the offered comestibles. Whilst Martin was stacking them into the boot of the car, Chloe asked.

"Can you walk into town from here?"

"You most certainly can," so they walked along the walkway, which ran along the side of the River Dee. The river was wide but not particularly deep, but it was swollen after the latest rain, causing the river Dee's water to tumble down much quicker over the rocks, some of which were still protruding through the fast-flowing currents and the forceful rapids before going under the old road bridge, then continued further down the river.

There were dozens of ducks preening themselves on the few rocks sticking above the water, also standing on the overhanging branches of the trees on the opposite side that were only just above the fast-flowing river.

Martin and Chloe continued towards the town, which wasn't that far, and then turned left onto the main road that passed through the picturesque village towards the old bridge, straddling the river. They peered over the parapet wall, looking upstream. An old steam engine was fired up, ready to haul a selection of ancient carriages out of the old Great Weston Railway station of Llangollen, all the way to Corwen on the heritage line.

"It's very picturesque; it's like stepping back into the 1950s." They didn't hang about long, as it was getting cold. On the way back to the car park, they stopped at a retro, second-hand clothing store where they sell all classic outdoor clothing; Chloe bought a waxed Barbour coat and hat. "Much more rustic," she said with a delighted smile. "More in keeping with your place," they then continued back to pick up the car, putting her purchases in the boot.

Martin started his Suzuki and pulled out of the line of parked cars. He noticed another car immediately started to follow him. He remembered what Chloe had told him about somebody following her. He said as he manoeuvred the vehicle out of the car park. "I'm going to turn left out of here instead of right. I have a feeling we have an audience behind us. You will need to brace yourself. He turned slowly left onto the main road, then took another left through one of the back streets of Llangollen, then right onto Bridge Street and pulled up at the traffic lights. The car following was two cars behind. The lights changed, so Martin turned right back onto the main A5 heading towards home. The car was following, still two cars back. Once out of the 30 miles per hour zone of Llangollen, he put his foot to the floor. Although not a fast car, it was still quite nippy. He pulled quickly away from the other cars, only to see whoever was following him overtake the two cars immediately behind. Martin knew the road well and wondered if the person driving behind knew exactly where Martin lived or not.

"This road, as you have found out, is very twisty, and going fast is not for the faint-hearted. Just up ahead, there is a very tight left-handed corner that's caught many an unsuspecting driver out," he said as they approached the bend in question. He changed down to third, keeping the revs well up, slipped around the bend, then accelerated out of the bend, changing back to fifth, speeding most of the way home. The lights of the car behind had momentarily disappeared, but as Martin went up his own drive a short while later and out of view from the road, he didn't know if the man had seen where he lived or not.

They removed all their purchases from the boot of the car. Some of the contents had spilled out of the bags, and most were lying in all the corners. Luckily, nothing, including the milk, had spilt out, and most had been a bit protected by Chloe's recently purchased Barbour coat. Once everything had been put away in the fridge, freezer, and cupboards, he decided to ring Evan, his friendly Welsh neighbour, asking if he would keep an eye open for a white Peugeot car. "I have just come back from Corwen," said Evan. "There is a white car parked on the drive, just off the main road where you used to park. We often get lovers parked there. They can be a bit of a nuisance, to be honest, but whether he's your man or not, I have no idea."

"Could you meet me down there in a few minutes? If he's on his own, it's probably the man I want a word with. He needs a bit of encouragement on leaving Wales and returning to wherever he emerged from."

It was getting dark when both men arrived from different directions at the bottom of the drive, which led up to Evan's house; Martin told Evan that this man had followed Chloe all the way from Cambridge. So, with a man on each side of the Peugeot and approached from the rear, they simultaneously threw both front car doors open. Evan grabbed the man out of his car, and they both pinned him against the bonnet of the car. "Who are you?" asked Martin in his non-threatening, calm voice, but the threat was there and very real.

"Private investigator, Dave Stibbins."

"Why were you following Professor Stone and then me?"

"Bin givn a wedge to find wer the Prof went."

"Why?"

"Caus I bin told to by some nob on the dog and bone."

While Evan held Stibbins, Martin walked around to the side of the vehicle, sat down in the passenger seat, and opened the glove compartment. Withdrawing a small piece of paper with Chloe's details and part of Martin's address, he placed it into his pocket and then returned to stand directly in front of Stibbins, then grabbed his lapel. "Who asked you to get this information and why?"

"Dunno, only ad a bone, thems ta ring me."

Letting him go, Martin said. "Clear off, tell them you couldn't get the information, and don't come back." Stibbins jumped into his car and screeched off.

"Do you know, I didn't understand a word that man said," confessed Evan. "What's a wedge and a bone/"

"Difficult, I must admit, comes from London," as an explanation, it's called rhyming slang. I don't know much about it myself. The bone, shortened from dog and bone, means the phone; a wedge is more complicated but means money, and a nob is slang for a posh person. But thanks for your help, Evan. I really appreciate it.

When Martin returned to his farmhouse, Chloe had cooked nothing more exotic than beans on toast, garnished with grated cheese on top, along with an opened bottle of Chateau *Aldi*. They talked about what they had been doing over the last few weeks. He didn't mention his recent visit to Rutland, the small box he had discovered there, or even depositing it into the bank.

Chloe then changed the conversation, which Martin was getting used to. "What do you want to achieve, or let me put it another way, what outcome do you want out of this discovery? Because you don't want to remove anything from the cave, nor do you want to sell anything."

"Do you know Chloe? I haven't the slightest idea what I am going to do. All I do know is I could have done without any of this hassle," and then added after a second or two of thought. "I have met you, which is quite nice," he said with a smile.

She looked away, slightly embarrassed. "All I can advise you to do now is take the book into the British Museum, and as quickly as you can. Unfortunately, we now have people who possibly have some of the papers that have my notes on them, which, as I have explained, were extremely revealing, if not disturbing. All these papers can be proved and have their provenance. It puts all previous guesswork that we have done for hundreds of years straight out the window. We have been told things that happened in our past, which, in fact, didn't happen. It may have been the church that bends things to their way of thinking, or it may have been how so-called academics read the situation. I have no idea, but what I do know is we have uncontroversial evidence to put everything straight, whether we like it or not. Also, as far as some facts we previously thought irrelevant or were made to fit what we wanted to hear, now could, in itself, be very dangerous."

"How do you mean dangerous?"

"There will be people out there in the real world who would give anything to get their hands on what you have got, and wouldn't give a damn how they got it. We now know that for a fact, as somebody followed me first, then us, which in itself is upsetting. The speed at which they have set about getting information regarding where you live is incredible; not sure why they want these documents, whether for monetary gain, or to own something that old, but I can promise you, others will join in the hunt for those parchments; they are probably worth many millions of pounds."

"That doesn't help me out of my dilemma. Those documents or parchments, or whatever you want to call them, have been safely stored in that cave for over 1200 years. Only you and I know where they are. That's as long as you haven't told anybody."

"I haven't told anybody. I don't know exactly where they are anyway, other than up a mountain," she took a deep breath before she continued. "Anyway, let me tell you what further aspects I uncovered which Merlin was an eye witness to in those Anglo-Saxon times, and it's obvious the way he has described the relationship between Christians and everybody else, who were on the whole anti-Christian, but it brings their beliefs into question, and the further we delve into Merlin's book I am positive we will discover more. Then there are the dates. We can already discredit Offa for building the so-called dyke, and then there are the dates of the Witan, which in themselves are insignificant, but can also be, by their very nature, of great importance.

"What's the Witan?"

"AH! A history lesson is required - then I will reveal all. The first *Witan,* or *Witenagemot*, as it should be called, was held in 742 in a place called *Viroconium* in what was believed to be Shropshire. That information came directly from Merlin's hand and is spot on. He wrote *Primum conventum tenit tempore pengwern Scrobbesdurd,* the last bit meaning Shropshire, a direct translation from scrubland."

"Why at that place?" asked Martin, doing his best to keep abreast with this history lesson.

"I can only deduce that if you look at maps of old Roman pathways of England, they converge into or near Shrewsbury. The most likely place is Wroxeter, a Roman city just south of where Shrewsbury is now. The *witan,* which was called the council of *Clofesho* or *Clofeshoch,* which, amongst other things, was to elect *Beornred* as king of Mercia, a new successor to, or to replace, not sure which, *Aethelbald,* among those present was *Elisedd ap Gwylog* from Wales, also many Bishops and Archdeacons."

"Why did they want to oust a King?"

"Well, Saint Boniface wrote to *Aethelbald* for various dissolute and irreligious acts. Don't forget that the church for those who worshipped was very strong at that time. If you wanted to go to heaven, you did what the church told you, which would include Kings, well, in fact, especially Kings. The problem was when *Aethelbald* came to the throne, both Wessex and Kent, which abutted Mercia, were ruled by stronger Kings. Within fifteen years, the contemporary chronicler *Bede* describes *Aethelbald* as ruling all of England south of the river Humber. Now, how did *Bede* get his information? He sent out people or agents to gather it. The more I go through Merlin's accounts, the more I doubt *Bede's* version of life in those days. I can't remember when he published *Historica ecclesiastica gentis anglorum,* but Bede died in 735, *so* there are many discrepancies in dates, i.e. you can't write about something when you are dead, so how did *Bede* know anything about the council of *Clofesho,* and there is no mention in *Bede's* History of its people regarding the *Witan,* but what has happened is people have put two and two together, and now with Merlin's account they don't even make 'three', there was always a mystery or a controversy over the *Witan,* Merlin has now turned that on its head. "

"So where is the mystery?"

"There is no mystery as far as Merlin was concerned. He was there and wrote what he saw. He says that Saint Boniface never wrote to *Aethelbald* that he sent men to murder him to prove and show these self-elected kings who were the boss, 'the church.' It didn't happen then, but it did later on; he was killed by his own bodyguards, and then *Beornred* took his place. So again, you have the church murdering people, which a lot of religious citizens will not take kindly to, especially when a Saint is involved."

"Sounds as if you have been very busy. Did you manage to translate everything before you were robbed?"

"There was a bit more to go, but the thief took everything I had translated. However, we have only copied parts of the book. There will be more to uncover, I am absolutely certain, but the more I think about it, there will be people who would not like that information to be aired in public."

"Such as who?"

"Staunch Catholics and very religious people, for starters, some academics who have written a thesis on parts of what we have discovered, which makes their thesis obsolete."

Chapter Twelve

The following day, after first visiting Professor Stone, Police Sergeant Roy Greisley was on a different shift again. So, at 1300 hrs, he was sitting in front of his computer writing up his report on the call out to Professor Stone the night before, and the subsequent paper they had found against a wheelie bin. As he read through that particular document again, it made him very uncomfortable. If this one random page revealed this amount of information, what would the rest divulge, and would they also be questionable against the Christian faith?

So, while debating all these particulars, he decided to just put generic words and phrases in to explain the literature found. He thought that it would be better rather than to describe in detail what was stolen from Professor Stone's flat.

The statement taken and filed by a young inspector about Mr. Patel at the convenience store was inconclusive and did not help, as their CCTV had been damaged a few days earlier and would either be repaired or replaced. Mr. Patel couldn't remember any one particular individual who visited his off-licence.

The sergeant grabbed his hat, shouted for Constable Parker to join him, and returned to Fulbourn to question Mr. S. Gibson again. They realised the house and grounds were in a very poor state of repair as they pulled up outside his house. It hadn't looked quite so bad in the dark, and again, they banged on the oak outside front door. Mr. Gibson opened the door just a few inches, "What now?" being his greeting, which was obviously his normal demeanour. *How does somebody like him get to hold the privileged job he has?* The police sergeant thought.

"Good afternoon, sir," replied the sergeant as sarcastically as he could manage. We have reasonable cause to believe you stole papers that hold valuable information that don't belong to you, so under section 17 of the Police and Criminal Act 1984, it permits us to search your premises. Therefore, I would ask you to sit on this chair while we carry out the search," he indicated to a chair that happened to be in the hallway. They searched the kitchen and lounge and then turned to Gibson's study, finding a laptop computer, and displayed on the screen was another sheet. That was just like the one they had found outside the professor's flat. "Can you tell me anything about this, Mr. Gibson?" as the constable led Gibson into the room.

"Downloaded it from the net," was his instant reply.

"Not helpful," said the sergeant. "I want more," and sat back on the swivel chair and waited. After a few moments of stony silence, the young constable turned the computer towards him while standing beside his sergeant and plied his knowledge to what else was on the computer. There were five further similar sheets; he continued looking into the computer's data, realising quickly that there was what looked like revolting porn material. Before he could see too much, the sergeant turned to the young constable and said. "Pack everything in evidence bags, constable, including this computer and every paper you can see." Then, he turned to Gibson to caution him, "You do not have to say anything. But it may harm your defence if you do not mention when questioned something that you later rely on in court. Anything you do say may be given in evidence. Do you understand, Mr Gibson?" Once this was achieved, they then put Gibson in the back of the police car and drove back to the police station, the bursar complaining all the way there whilst sitting uncomfortably in the back with his hands in handcuffs behind him.

Stanley Gibson was seated in an interview room after they had removed his handcuffs and given him a cup of tea, while the details were given to the inspectors to sort out the paperwork and the tech guys to sort through the computer to ascertain what they could charge Gibson with. Prior to handing the computer over, Sergeant Greisley installed it on his desk, booted it up, printed the five copies that he had previously seen, and then handed over the computer to the techno, saying, "Try and find out how the five sheets of scripts got there or, indeed, if they came off the net, which I doubt. CID will want copies of those papers, as we don't know if they are a hoax or factual. Also, I believe there is child porn that's been downloaded onto his computer."

The papers Sergeant Greisley had purloined were very interesting indeed, once he had time to study them, notwithstanding the piece he was holding in front of him, with the words Professor Stone had written underneath most of the original wording, to make it at least understandable English. Unfortunately, it revealed little to him as it would to an academic; nonetheless, the bits he could understand were about Christianity, the King of Mercia, and many things he couldn't even pronounce, let alone understand. The longer he studied the sheets, the more he became aware of what was being conveyed. He was writing down the words he could understand in the order they came off the papers. 'Elimination of all non-Christian people was one, 'moving any non-Christians into Wales was another,' which is what the other paper said about building Offa's dyke. He sat back after a while, considering what to do. He couldn't approach anybody with more knowledge about this type of thing, as they would enquire where he got these sheets from in the first place. He would have to study all these papers far more closely before deciding what to do personally. As far as he was concerned, he would want to destroy the original defamatory material. Wherever it was, he was not going to stand by and let anybody slag off anything about Christianity.

Once the inspectors had gathered all the information, both from the sergeant and the technical guys, they entered the interview room where Mr. Gibson had been impatiently waiting for nearly 3 hours. He was not a happy man, shouting at the inspectors as soon as they entered the room. They sat down on the opposite side of the desk from Gibson and waited for him to calm down. "Sorry to keep you waiting, sir. Have you had a cup of tea? Well, we will make a start."

Detective Inspector Brown was not one to listen to people raving for no apparent reason, switched on the recorder, which was in the corner of the room. They introduced themselves, reminded Gibson he was still under caution, and reiterated he was entitled to a solicitor if he so desired.

"I have done nothing wrong, so do your worst," he replied, very agitated.

"First, can you tell me where you obtained these papers?" Brown asked, tapping the copies of papers in the file in front of him; he turned them and pushed the pile towards Gibson.

"Off the internet," came back the sneering reply.

"I'm going to ignore that last remark and ask you again, Mr. Gibson, where did you obtain these papers? Our technical lads tell me they were scanned into your computer, not downloaded. We require **all** the originals back by the way, but as yet, we believe you have done anything with them, not that I know what you were going to do with them in the first place, also, what you didn't know was the gentleman who owns the original material, only allowed professor Stone to have copies on the expressed condition she put nothing on her computer."

"Now, although all her research is carried out on these machines, she has obeyed the instructions to the letter, so before I lose my temper, I will ask you nicely again: where did you get them from?"

"I only borrowed them for the information they may contain. They could just as easily be a hoax, and I didn't want our college funds being wasted. I was also interested in what Professor Stone was doing."

"You are a bursar at one of the finest universities in the world; it pains me to ask you if you really know the definition of borrow?"

"Well, I wouldn't have kept them if that is what you are implying."

"Sir, I am not even going to answer that. Do you know a Mr. Stibbins?"

"Who?"

"Mr. Gibson, we now know you arranged a private investigator, a certain Mr. Stibbins, to follow Professor Stone back to the owner's property of the said papers. Stibbins was apprehended by this gentleman and his next-door neighbour, and they asked him to return whence he came, London, we believe; I don't know if they are the exact words used, but that is what the gentleman has told us."

"I asked Stibbins to follow Chloe Stone. Yes, I wanted to know where these papers had come from. I would then have approached the person in question to see if we could come to some financial arrangement, that's if they are authentic."

"Are these papers worth anything in monetary value then?"

"Intrinsic value only, I should think if the originals are genuine," said Gibson, trying to devalue and divert attention from their true worth, of what could be something worth many millions.

At that point, another inspector put his head around the interview room door and asked if Brown had a minute. They had just come from the tech guys and told Brown, "We have retrieved all the original copies, wiped his computer, and also checked all his other equipment, so if you want to let him go, that's fine. Oh! The pornography, although not nice, isn't child pawn, and by the way, and for what it's worth, in my opinion, those papers look like a load of bollocks to me."

Detective Inspector Brown returned to the interview room and told Gibson everything he had just been told. "A word of warning, though, if we find anything appertaining to this episode on the internet, we will re-arrest you immediately, so you can now go. It will be up to the CPS if they want to charge you for breaking and entering," with that concluded. Brown gathered up all the papers and departed from the interview room. A constable had to drive Gibson home after he did some complaining about having no money with him to even get a bus back.

When Stanley Gibson returned home, he decided to ring Stibbins on his mobile; it was answered on the second ring. "I paid you to follow Professor Stone just to find out where she went, not to get into a dialogue with all and sundry. Why did you tell those people who you were following?"

"Tha trewff is, aint nowt else I cud say istha, tha cawt me red anded by thems I wus follerin, er boyfriend enyways."

"Do you know where they live?"

"Yeh, if yu's wants it, yu's guna pays me bill first, an it's gonup, cus of tha azzal iv's ad."

"Tell me how much I owe you, and I will put a cheque in the post."

"Do ya fink I am soft in the ed or summut, bring me a monkey in cash ta the fox an ound pub tamorra nigt."

"£500, that's double what we agreed, and daylight robbery. Do you think I'm made out of money?"

"Tekit or leevit, see ya tamorra nigt," the phone went dead.

The following day, Gibson withdrew £500 from his building society bank account and went along the road to the Fox and Hounds public house. He sat there for some time and drank far more alcohol than he was used to. Stibbins eventually turned up, and Gibson handed over the agreed amount in a brown envelope. In return, Stibbins gave him a small piece of paper with an address on it, then gave him a very brief description of where the house was situated.

"It would be difficult to find if you ain't follern im," and with that, Stibbins departed.

Gibson then went back home to plan how he was going to obtain the original papers; he knew they would be worth many millions of pounds on the open market.

Stanley Gibson set off for North Wales the following day. He had never been to this part of the British Isles and had to admit and admire the rugged beauty and scenic vistas, especially all along the Dee Valley after leaving Llangollen. However, the journey took him a lot longer than he anticipated it would. Basically, it was further than he thought. He was not only given the address but was told to pull up in a lay-by a few hundred yards past Lidiart-y-parc, which he was doing now, thinking how on earth you pronounced some of these village names, wondering not for the first time what they all meant.

Chapter Thirteen

The drive to the owner's property, of whom he still didn't know the name, was at the other end of the lay-by. He knew he had the right house; its name was clearly visible at the bottom of his drive. He got out of the car quickly, realising it was very cold. The only extra layer he had that happened to be in the boot of the car was his old gabardine mac. He quickly put it on, thinking about it. This was the only outdoor clothing he owned. Gibson was not one for outdoor pursuits, but was much more at home in the betting shop to back his horses. He walked the short distance to the driveway, very conscious that he would be immediately recognised by Chloe Stone if she happened to drive out of the driveway.

Once he left the drive, although he wore country brogue shoes, they had smooth leather soles, which was not ideal for that terrain. Consequently, he was sliding all over the place and was exacerbated by everything being wet. He clambered up the embankment using small trees and shrubs to pull himself along. Then, he settled down amongst the vegetation, which was all in a state of lying bare and dormant; consequently, there was little coverage, making him a bit more exposed than he would have liked. As he was slightly more elevated than the house and barns, he could see their cars parked haphazardly across the courtyard. Therefore, he knew they were both at home. He made himself as comfortable as possible and waited. They would have to go out at some time, in theory anyway.

"Let's have a break from all this," said Martin, feeling in a garrulous mood.

"Where would you like to go? Seaside, Bala Lake, or a walk along the river?"

"Do you know, I haven't been to the seaside for….Oh! Must be 20 years. Let's take a run out there. I will treat you to fish and chips. It's now coming up midday. How long will it take?"

"About an hour to get there; the best fish and chips in Wales are at Barmouth. Grab your hat. Let's go." They put their warmest clothes and boots on, picked Raffles up off his hotbed and put him out, locked up the house, got into the Suzuki, and shot off to the coast.

They departed so fast that Gibson nearly missed them driving off. He had also started to doze off, even though, as uncomfortable and as cold as he was, all he could think about was the potential gain when he sold these papers. He scrambled back down the embankment, jumped into his car, and drove up to the old farmhouse. Wherever they were going, it would be a minimum of an hour, as this was such a remote area, so he decided he must leave the house at no more than 1 o'clock, while looking at his watch. He walked around the outside of the house, trying windows and doors, but nothing was open. He grabbed a lump of slate and threw it as hard as he could at the back door glass; it cracked, but the slate bounced off. Bugger.

He threw it again and again. It took 8 throws to smash it completely. By the time he had got himself through the top half of the door, ripped his Mac in the process, and entered the house, he was exhausted, with perspiration running down the sides of his face. At least there were no alarms. Nearly half an hour had gone by, he thought, looking at his watch again. He wandered through the house, wondering where the owner would have left the original papers. They would almost certainly be vellum or some sort of parchment. He was excited at the thought of feeling something that old.

He found the old box containing Martin's family tree, but discarded it as irrelevant. He eventually came across Professor Stone's briefcase, which was an old-fashioned type with a leather strap. He returned to the kitchen, cut the strap with a sharp knife, and delved into the case. There were more of the same sheets with notes, but no parchments. He folded them up and put them into his inside pocket. Then, he had one more look around, moving pictures and turning over some of the furniture. He even tested the carpets, but all were secured down, and in the end, he decided they must be either cleverly hidden or they weren't in the farmhouse, then left a bit disappointed by the way he had entered.

Well, that was a waste of time, he thought, driving back to Cambridge, musing but thinking more clearly, they wouldn't have them left in the house. It was rather silly to think he might find anything, but one thing was obvious: he needed some sort of specialist help. Now, what sort of help? I think some sort of persuasion is needed to obtain them.

Martin and Chloe arrived back at Martin's farm at 4 o'clock, just as it was getting dark, having had a delightful few hours together. Martin noticed the break-in immediately. He unlocked the door, and both of them ran around the property looking for what had been stolen or damaged. It didn't take long to discover Chloe's briefcase with the strap cut through, and realised all the papers were missing. The computer was still in place, as was everything else. Raffles was quite pleased with himself as he had returned to the house through the broken window and was back on his throne. Martin looked at the cat. "I hope you had nothing to do with this break-in," then rang the Cambridge police and asked to speak to Sergeant Roy Greisley, they replied. "He will be able to ring you back in ten minutes. He was due to start his shift shortly. And can you tell me what it is regarding, and your telephone number?"

After briefly telling the person on the other end what the situation was, he made the second phone call. It was reported to the local police force as it was a local crime. It was answered in their bilingual answering phone, which Martin was now becoming used to. He wondered how many people, even those born in Wales and actually living in Wales, could only speak Welsh and wouldn't or couldn't understand any English. However, it was answered after a few clicks; it must have gone through to a different department, he thought. "P.C. Roberts, how can I help you?" Came the lovely sing-song voice.

"My name is Martin Ambrose," and gave them his address. "We have just been broken into and burgled," he told them. "I wondered if you could send someone around."

"There will be somebody there shortly," said the constable. "There are two of our local lads just around the corner from you, dealing with another incident; I will give them a call."

While they were waiting for the long arm of the law to turn up, Chloe made a cup of tea for each of them. Martin looked into the barn for a piece of plywood to insert into position. It would be temporary while they rang up and sorted out double glazing. While he was rummaging around, the landline rang, so Chloe answered it. It was Sergeant Greisley returning their call. She related what had happened, then added that the only person who knew anything about those papers, which were the only things stolen, was the original thief. The sergeant had to agree and promised to make some enquiries and get back to them.

A short time later, two police officers arrived in a

Nissen 4 x 4, the normal mode of transport for North Wales. Again, Martin and Chloe explained that the only thing that the thief had taken was the same type of papers, which had also been stolen in Cambridge. The police officers could see the damage to the glass themselves, and all agreed that the cost of replacing the glass would not cover the insurance excess. "What were the papers that were stolen? Are they something out of the ordinary, or worth a lot of money?" the WPC asked as she took out her notebook and wrote a few details down.

So, they went through the same routine as with the Cambridge Constabulary. "These are copies of the original parchments. Thank God they are in a very secure place. As far as what they are worth, the paper would only cost a few pence; what is written on them is potentially groundbreaking, the original parchment would possibly be worth in excess of £10 million."

As the young WPC started to write, she stopped dead, "Errr, how many noughts in 10 million?"

"Do you own these originals, sir?" said the other constable as his colleague was stumped for words or noughts in her case."

"Yes."

The constable said, "When we get back to the station, we will ring Cambridge, but what I cannot understand is whoever took these papers, and I agree with you, it is highly probable that it will be the same person. He must either be desperate or an idiot. They must know we would put two and two together. However, I notice you have no burglar alarm of any type, although crime around these parts is rare, I think you could do with some sort of anti-theft system of some sort, and possibly a camera or two about the place, if we had an image of whoever it was, that would have been end of story for him, or her," so after a few placatory words and a cup of coffee, they left after leaving a number they recommended for a security firm.

Chapter Fourteen

After Police Sergeant Roy Greisley had spoken both to the local constabulary in Wales and to the professor on the phone, who was also back in North Wales with possibly the owner of these said papers. He sat back in his chair and thought, these papers are copies of the originals, and not as he first thought, a hoax, for someone to go all the way to North Wales that quickly and try to retrieve them, they were obviously out for the money they were worth.

So, whatever was written down and then translated must also be factual, no matter what he thought at first was right or wrong. But as far as he was concerned, the information being conveyed was not what he was prepared to be resigned to, which, in Roy's own mind and beliefs, must be destroyed. Although Professor Stone is translating them in Cambridge, the originals must be in North Wales as the owner lives there. There is no way he would keep them in a bank, as most of the banks had shut in Wales over the last few years. Therefore, it must be hidden in his house or fairly close to where the owner lives. First, he needed to grab his constable and take a trip to see the bursar again. The bursar must be really thick to go and retrieve the translated copies. Not only was he the prime suspect, but he was the only suspect now. Whether he returned back home with them, or had taken them somewhere else was open to debate, but he had to start somewhere. Putting the wind up the bursar was as good as anything.

It didn't take long to drive out to Gibson's house, only to find him not at home. They walked around the house, but it was definitely empty of occupants. "Now where?" said the young constable.

"We will go to the university; the stupid bugger would take them there to hide them and must have a deluded mind to think we wouldn't work that out."

"Which one? There are dozens of them."

"If it's to do with old Languages, then MML, Modern and Medieval languages, I think it's part of Clare College. Look it up on your smartphone."

The constable scrolled down through the entries. "Here it is, Sedgwick Avenue," they both got back into the police car and shot off.

They couldn't park anywhere near to the entrance, and ended up parking and having to walk quite a fair distance to get there. They were greeted by the porter as soon as they entered through the archway leading into the college. "We would like to speak to Mr. Stanley Gibson."

"Have you an appointment, sirs?" the porter, who, although the title was slightly unassuming, was an important member of the staff to any university college, his paramount importance was the welfare of all the students. Unfortunately, not having had much contact with addressing such lowly in the pecking order, as far as he was concerned, as policemen, he thought they should be discouraged rather than made welcome. "No, not as far as I am aware.".

"We are on official business; we need to have a word with him at the earliest. Could you check if he is here? We would like to ask him a few questions."

The porter went through a small doorway that led to a very small room. Through a little window, they could see the porter talking on the phone to somebody. After a few moments, he reappeared. "I have not seen that particular gentleman today, err, sirs."

"Is it possible to enter these grounds without anybody knowing?"

The porter looked up to the sky and said, in a very dry, unhelpful way, as if he had a thousand other things to do, "Probably, sirs, I wouldn't know."

"Will you convey a message to him when you do see him, or if you can communicate in a way that would procure a response, to get in touch with us? Here are our telephone numbers," the sergeant said, handing him a card with all the local police details on.

The porter took the proffered card as if it were contaminated with anthrax. "Sirs," with a small nod of his head to indicate he had finished any further dialogue with these inferior subjects, he disappeared inside his little room.

****

Detective Inspector Jeff Brown had accomplished being a DI by slow, methodical thought processes and not rushing about like the younger generation seemed to do. Now, at 48, it was as high up in rank as he was likely to get. He was a big, solid man with chiselled features and would tolerate most things, but never incompetence. He was sitting in his little cupboard, known as an office, studying the copies from the supposedly original parchment or documents. These had been handed to him, and Professor Stone's translations were under most of the words. Also, he was now considering and mulling over the break-in at both the professor's house and one he had just heard about at the owner's property. Presumably to obtain the originals, but something as rare and obviously quite valuable, the last place they would be kept is someone's house.

He had now spoken to North Wales police about the break-in there. With the exception of a smashed window and the paper copies that Professor Stone had in her briefcase, they had little else to say. They, like him, wondered if these scraps of paper could be worth what they say they are valued at. He thought it might be advantageous to find out himself what all the fuss was about, and why these papers were so important. He decided in the end to ring an old friend at Scotland Yard who worked on the fraud squad, so maybe he could point him in the right direction, at least. Mike Wilcox answered on the second ring, and after a few felicitations,

Brown briefly outlined what he had rung him about. "You want somebody in the art and antiques unit, old son. I'm not sure they deal with the type of stuff you have described, but they could at least give you some guidance. I will put you through. You look after yourself."

Again, the phone was answered quickly. "DI Roger Wilson," came a brusque reply.

"Roger, have you a few minutes? I have a problem." DI Brown briefly told the Scotland Yard inspector the situation and went on. "They could be copies of some genuine parchments, which we have also been told could be worth many millions of pounds, as you and I know, there are many people willing to kill for that sort of money."

"Give me a clue as to what is written on them, will you, Jeff? It sounds quite intriguing. Tell me, are these copies from the originals? Photocopied, or have they been copied out by hand?"

They have been copied out by hand, possibly from original papers, with the translation above or below each word. There are lots of gaps and bracketed bits. To be honest, I don't understand much of it. They write about the first Witan and Offa's dyke. There is much more, but as I said, I am not conversant with even the translated parts. All I am doing is trying to get a handle on it, just to see if it's worth spending time and resources on, or is it one big hoax."

"OK, the first *Witan* was in the 8th century, *Offa's* dyke was built in the 9th, and any original parchment or manuscript from that era should be in the British Museum. They are classified as antiquity. That's the first thing. Now I am just pondering," the line went silent for some moments as he was obviously thinking. "Whoever wrote originally about the W*itan* and *Offa's* dyke couldn't or is unlikely to have been around for both events. The time frame is out. However, if it was the same person who wrote about these things, there must be something else to go with it. Who claims they are from the genuine article?"

"A Professor Chloe Stone; ever heard of her?"

"Funnily enough, I have. I think she is an expert in old languages at the MML. Give them a ring, or better still, go get her opinion and ask her to put anything she says in writing." And yes, you could have a potential problem regarding protecting the originals. Try to ensure the museum is where they end up because, after all, that is our heritage. It belongs to us and needs looking after.

"OK, I will do that, but going back to what you just said, you are quite right in saying there must be more to it. These parchments claim that the Offa's dyke was built 70 odd years before we are led to believe it was built, and wasn't built by Offa at all, it was built to keep non-Christians in Wales, or words to that effect, and there is a mountain of these sheets similar to those I have here."

"Bloody hell, mate! That will go down a storm with

the church. Look, Jeff, do as I have suggested. You are in Cambridge; go and have a word with Professor Stone or somebody similar, find out exactly what you are dealing with, and get them to verify if you are dealing with a hoax or not. They will know. The originals would be classed as British antiquities. I take it the authorities are not yet privy to them, but once they do know, they will move heaven and earth to protect them and will stamp on anybody who gets in their way, including you, so cover your arse, mate, and do it quickly."

"Are they worth much, or is it just the antiquity value?"

"On the open market, the originals could be worth many millions. One sheet of parchment from that era is virtually priceless. I know hundreds of villains in London who would quite willingly kill to get their hands on them, especially for the sort of money they would fetch, and wouldn't give a monkey about splitting them up. I wish you the very best of luck, old son. You are going to need it. Speak to you again, Jeff. Bye," and he hung up.

After talking to Roger Wilson, he got through to Cambridge University. He told them who he was and who he wanted to talk to, so they put him through to the MML. "Doctor Phillip Langton here, how can I help you?" were his first words. So, Inspector Brown yet again repeated what he had told Roger Wilson to Doctor Langton, "The person who can best help you isn't here at the moment. If you bring what you have now, I can have a quick look and try to point you in the right direction. We are on Sedgewick Avenue."

Brown turned up half an hour later and was shown into Philip Langton's office. They shook hands and sat down opposite the doctor's desk. On the desk was a sign that read Doctor Philip Langton, with more letters after his name than the alphabet. Brown proffered the sheets onto the table, turned them to face the doctor, and pushed them towards him.

As the Doctor glanced down at the sheets of paper laid out in front of him through his half-rimmed glasses, noticing the old script with the neat translated words beneath, and commented, "These have already been translated. Looks very much like Professor Stone's hand. I would think she has had her work cut out to cover this amount," Brown thought he spoke rhetorically, so he said nothing. While the Doctor continued scrutinising what had been handed to him, he took up a pencil and paper and wrote down a few notes. At one stage, he got up out of his chair, went across his office to retrieve a book off the shelf, examined it, replaced it, and sat down again, looking absolutely bewildered. After an age, he looked up at the inspector and said. "There are many gaps in translation, mainly because no words match the modern lexicon. What you have here is ground-shattering. Tell me, how much more is there? Do you know?"

"From what I am led to believe, there is much more."

"Well, I can say with some certainty," said the Doctor.

"If these are copied from originals, there would be little doubt the originals are genuine, and if Chloe Stone is involved with these, there would be a very good reason for her not to already have them in the British Museum. Do you know if they know of their existence, by the way?"

"No, I don't. Should we contact them?"

"Leave it with me, inspector. I will contact them on your behalf if you wish. I know one or two people who work in the museum. I will have a quiet word. If you say too much, they will swarm everywhere, and that is probably not what Chloe wants. I am sure she will have everything in hand, but thinking about it, the best course of action would be for me to talk to Chloe first." After telling Brown all he needed to know and more he didn't want to know, they shook hands and parted.

Chapter Fifteen

Sergeant Roy Greisley was due a fair amount of leave, so he decided to take three days off from work, telling his wife he was going walking in the Snowdonia National Park. A little puzzled by her husband's sudden decision to go away, especially in the middle of winter, she found a few days on her own with the girls seemed an appealing break from him. He had busily checked all his equipment and had stored it methodically away in the boot of his car, ready for an early start the following morning.

The ensuing day proved to be very cold but with a crystal-clear sky, so once he had finished his breakfast and scraped the ice from the windscreen, he set off, after previously setting his satnav for his destination. The journey was uneventful and rather tedious, so after sitting behind the steering wheel for far too many hours, he arrived at his pre-booked destination of the Berwyn Arms in a place called Glyndyfrdwy at just after 1 o'clock. But even after asking how you pronounce such a place, he would not be able to repeat it. It was conveniently located, only a short distance from the address taken off a very unhappy bursar regarding the gentleman who owned the original works. All those papers had quite upset him, mainly because they knocked Christianity and the church; he felt compelled to destroy anything that would rock his feelings or his faith.

After clocking into the Inn and depositing his bags into the room he would be staying in, he decided to go for a bit of a stroll. He wrapped up warmly and set off for a walk around the area. Greisley walked along the road, which was the A5. Although the road was busy, it was not unduly so. This, he had found out, was because the new expressway, which was a more direct route to Holyhead and was far faster to travel on, had far fewer small villages to negotiate for the big lorries heading to Ireland via that port, where the vast amount of traffic would be going.

Walking along, he had to admit it was a beautiful part of the world. He glanced over the stone wall: the Dee valley with the river snaking away into the distance, the Llangollen heritage railway running along the side of it, interspersed with rugged fields, along with the ubiquitous sheep. On the opposite side of the road where he was walking, a small stream tumbled over rocks, went under the road, and continued down to join the river. Mountains in the distance completed this wonderful picture-postcard view. He had looked up the area before setting out; this was the very place where the last real Prince of Wales, named Owain Glyndŵr, had lived. In fact, only a few miles up the road, before setting out on his campaign to remove the English from Wales, he gained many supporters en-route. The crusade had failed. Owain Glyndŵr was never seen again, and consequently, the Welsh suffered persecution for a hundred years thereafter.

The address he had purloined was further along this road than he thought and just after another unpronounceable village, but he detected where the entrance to the farmhouse drive was. Then, after a short recce, he wandered back the way he had come.

By the time he had arrived back, it was turning dark and getting even colder. He sat by a roaring fire with a pint of Marston's 'Owd Roger', listening to two old farmers arguing in Welsh. He couldn't understand a word they were saying, but it was quite entertaining nevertheless.

After a while, he went and had an agreeable dinner. While he ate his dinner, he thought about the man who owned these parchments. He still did not even know his name, but never for one moment did he think he would leave them hanging around his own property. If not there, then where? The nearest bank was Wrexham, which was 25 miles away, not particularly handy. Where else? He felt sure there must be somewhere else the gentleman would find handy. He also wondered if these papers had been stored in his house since they were written. Whenever that was, he hadn't a clue. All he knew for certain was that they were very old and were defamatory to his faith.

Stanley Gibson, meanwhile, had managed to get into his rooms at Clare College without being detected. It wasn't difficult; boys had been entering and departing from this college for many years without any problems. He had now copied down everything that Professor Stone had translated, coming to the conclusion that the originals would be worth an absolute fortune. Now, if he wasn't able to locate them himself — as he never had those types of skills — in fact, that entire trip was a waste of time and effort. It needed somebody with a little more of a persuasive technique, far more than he was able to deliver, that was for sure, and certainly more than Stibbins. But Stibbins might know somebody of that calibre.

He rang Stibbins to ask if he knew anybody who could help locate the original parchments. "Possibly with a slightly more eloquent and coercive approach than either of the two of them had?" he added, then thought Stibbins might not understand that sort of English. But he must have understood his dialogue because after a lot of ums and ahs, Stibbins begrudgingly gave Gibson a telephone number. He rang it immediately. It was answered by a curt, "Yes." Gibson told the person on the other end of the line what he wanted.

"Meet me tomorrow night at the Old Swan," and the line went dead.

The following night, as instructed, Gibson was supping his second pint when he was tapped on the shoulder, and somebody bent down behind his right ear.

"You're wanted outside now."

The bursar turned around to see who had spoken to him and saw the large shoulders and the back of a man disappearing through the doorway.

Leaving his half-finished pint, he did up his coat and exited the same way. Once outside, he looked about him and could only see parked cars. A hand grabbed underneath his arm and frog-marched him to the far corner of the car park, then unceremoniously shoved him into the back seat of a Range Rover. There were no lights on, so Gibson couldn't see who he was talking to.

"You called me. Who gave you, my phone number?"

"David Stibbins, that's if you are the person who can help me?"

"First, destroy the phone number. Second, what is it you want me to do?"

"Locate and retrieve some 8th-century parchments. They will be very delicate and need careful handling."

"Are they valuable? Because I charge 30% of what they are worth when we recover them, plus £5,000 up front for expenses."

"Can you guarantee getting them delivered?"

"Never failed yet."

"Where do I take the money?"

"You don't. Somebody will collect it from your house tomorrow night, and an address where these parchments are kept, or a starting point anyway. So, how much are they worth?"

"Upwards of a million pounds. They must be in perfect condition when I get them, or they are not worth anything."

After giving him his address, he just said, "Now clear off. Somebody will pick up the five grand tomorrow night."

It was a few days later when two men approached Martin at his farmhouse while the double-glazing men were repairing the back door window. They pushed their way by them and into the kitchen, where Martin was making tea for the glaziers. Martin, remaining his usual calm self, turned and asked, "How can I help you?" but underneath, he was annoyed that anybody should barge into his house.

"We've come to collect some old parchments," said one.

"What the hell are you talking about? I have no parchments."

"Look mate, we ain't com eer to go up Snowdon. We com eer ta collect som ald parchment, so and em over," blurted the second man.

"Get out or I will call the police."

The two glaziers, hearing raised voices and a sort of conversation, came into the kitchen and stood behind the two men.

"Everything alright, Mr. Ambrose?"

"Yes, these men are just leaving."

With that, the two men turned and went out of the house, one adding, "You will be sorry you never gave them to us." They got back into their car and drove back down the drive.

"Do you know who those two were?" asked one of the glaziers, taking his tea as Martin handed it to him.

"I have no idea, but I have a feeling I haven't seen the last of them. I am beginning to get used to people breaking in or demanding and trying to steal things I haven't got."

As soon as the glaziers left, Martin rang the police and told them about the threatening behaviour in his own kitchen by two men.

"Somebody will call round to see you presently," they told him.

The back door fixed, Martin thought he needed some extra security like the first policeman had told him, so he rang a firm that specialised in home security alarms and cameras. He told them that his house had been broken into, and now two men had turned up and threatened him. The nice thing about living in North Wales is that it has such a sparse population, things tend to get done quickly….well, most things.

The police turned up an hour later, walked around the farmhouse and yard, gave advice on how to make his home more secure, took a statement, and apologised for not being any more helpful. Martin told the police officer that when he had discovered the break-in, the officer who came then, told him he needed better security and had only just got around to doing something about it.

An hour after the police had gone, the security firm turned up. After some constructive discussions, they fitted three cameras, as well as a few sensors connected back to a hidden monitor in one of his kitchen cupboards. They promised to get better and more sophisticated night vision cameras, and the burglar alarms fitted as soon as they could get them. After the security firm had gone, Martin remembered seeing an old army pistol in one of his father's old boxes. There was no ammunition, but a gun can be a good persuader, so he went in search for it.

Chapter Sixteen

After much deliberation whether or not to ring Chloe, as he wanted, or maybe he needed, to talk to someone, in the end, he dismissed it as he didn't want her upset, and went to see his friendly neighbour Evan.

He was greeted with much bonhomie, a cup of tea, and a slice of his wife's bara brith, something he was getting very fond of, along with Welsh cakes.

"I have come for some advice and probably some help. I have very few people I know with the skills I need," Martin started. "The thing is, Evan, I own something very rare and valuable." Then he thought for a minute. "Let me put it another way, I know where something is that is virtually priceless, nay, is priceless. As far as I know, I am the only person able to access it." Again, Martin thought he was making no sense whatsoever.

Evan and his wife looked sympathetically at Martin. "Have another cup of tea and another slice of cake, take a deep breath and start again," she said encouragingly.

"OK, by default, which I won't go into just now, other people have found out I own this valuable commodity. Do you remember Evan, when that person on your driveway arrived, and we encouraged him to go back where he had come from? Well, that was the start of it. Anyway, I had intended to keep everything a secret, but things have now got out of hand. In fact, they are now escalating to a dangerous level. I want to move this valuable object into the British Museum, but I cannot do it by myself. In the last week, my house has been broken into, searched, and today I was threatened by two men in my own kitchen."

Mrs. Griffiths was outraged that such a thing had happened around here. "Who were these people?" she asked.

"I have no idea, other than they are probably from either London or Cambridge. Now, at this stage, I don't want to say too much about what this object is, because so far, everybody who knows about it appears to be in danger, and I certainly don't want to put you two in that situation."

"Do you want my help to move it, retrieve it, or just suggestions on what to do?" asked Evan, eager to help his friend.

"To retrieve it in itself will be exceptionally difficult; also, it is very delicate and probably a bit awkward to move."

"Can it be boxed up?" Evan then added. "How big and heavy is it?"

Martin held his arms out to indicate roughly the size of the book, then added, "I can get a carpenter to manufacture a strong box, and get him to put strong straps on it to enable it to be carried on someone's back. I would think along with the box it would weigh, er, I don't know, er, 30 to 40 lbs," he said, scratching his head, thinking of pounds in weight rather than kilos. "Then we still have to get it to London, which may seem trivial, but with these other people watching my every move, it could be dangerous."

"So let me get this straight. This object could be boxed up, the box made along with shoulder straps to go, say, onto a fit and strong person's back?"

"With strong straps, I would think that would be achievable, yes."

Evan picked up his smartphone, pushed a few times with his stubby fingers on the face of it, and was soon talking to someone in Welsh. After a minute, he looked at Martin. "Could you get a box made up and ready by the day after tomorrow, and will this object remain safe till then?" he asked, still holding on to the phone.

Martin was taken aback by his sudden enthusiasm and assurance toward him. "The object will be safe. Whether I will be is debatable. I don't know about the carpenter, but I'm sure if I throw enough money at it, they should be able to accomplish it."

He spoke back into the phone in Welsh and then rang off. "That was my son Dafydd. He and his friend will be only too pleased to get this thing, whatever it is and wherever it is, and into the British Museum."

Martin was a bit taken aback by both the receptive way he had grasped the problem and the resolve to come up with the solution. "I really appreciate this, Evan. I was reticent to do anything before now, but with my hands tied behind my back, it was difficult to know what I was going to do. Are you sure your son won't mind? I certainly don't want anybody taking any risks."

"It's no problem. Dafydd will enjoy the challenge. He's in the army," he added proudly, and with that, the two men shook hands warmly. Martin gave Mrs. Griffiths a peck on the cheek and drove back to his farmhouse, a little relieved.

No sooner had he arrived back at his home than his landline phone was ringing. It was Chloe. "I have been ringing you for ages to tell you I have been contacted by David Langton from my department at the university, who told me the police, a Detective Inspector Brown to be precise, wants to know how genuine the papers he has got were. I asked him what was on the papers. He described the original batch that was stolen. Do you want me to ring him?"

He told Chloe, "I've decided to get the book into the British Museum as soon as possible, and to that end, I've got somebody willing to take it directly there. I am on a roll at the moment, so leave the inspector to me."

"Thank God for that. I will ring the museum and get them prepared. They hate surprises, and I know some of the staff there. I will leave you to the police then."

"Give me the police inspector's phone number. I will ring him as soon as I have sorted out another little problem."

Martin rang the carpenter he used for the renovation of his property, telling him what he wanted, not one box but two, identical and complete with some sort of strong shoulder straps and clasps.

"I can do them for next week," he said cheerfully, and gave him an estimate of how much it would cost.

"No, you don't understand, let me explain. These boxes are for some historical documents that have to be transferred to the British Museum. If I offer you double the estimate, in cash, can you do them for me tomorrow?"

The line went quiet for a few moments, then the carpenter said, "I can do my best. Do you want them brought up to your farm?"

"Yes, that would be great. I have two army guys coming to carry these valuable documents, which are what the boxes are for, and transfer them to the British Museum, possibly the day after tomorrow."

"Sounds like you have Dafydd and Gareth on your side. Word of warning, though, they are not just the army. They are in the SAS and are as hard as iron. I went to school with Dafydd. If he says he will get them into the British Museum, he will get them there. The boxes will be there by tomorrow night. I will have to oversize the straps, though. Both of those are man-mountains. Bye for now."

Martin was never surprised by how everybody knew everybody else in this part of the country. Then he rang the police inspector. Martin told him who he was and said, "How can I help you?"

"These papers, Doctor Langton tells me, he thinks are copied off the originals. Can you tell me some facts? Do you own the originals?"

"Difficult to give a yes or no answer without me sounding a loony. I am the only person who can get at them because of certain attributes I have. Also, because of the problems that are unfolding, we are going to try and get them into the British Museum the day after tomorrow."

"That is what I have been told by others you should do, and it sounds like an excellent solution to me. I believe your house has been broken into. I am assuming they are not kept at your house, but are these parchments, or whatever they are, safe?"

"Quite safe, I assure you. I have also been threatened by two men inside my own kitchen. That is why there is now more of an urgency in getting the parchments into the museum."

"I have spoken to a number of colleagues as well as this Doctor Langton. They all agree that if the originals are genuine, and what you have told me seems to confirm that, those original documents are virtually priceless. Also, with something that rare and important, if you need help, you must notify me, or even if you have any more dealings with these people. They are now obviously trying to gain access to these papers, or whatever they are called. And lastly, will you let me know even if you don't go ahead with this transfer, and contact me when you are expecting to have completed the journey to London?" He gave Martin his personal mobile number and then rang off.

The following day, Martin was woken by a loud bang downstairs. He glanced at the bedside clock.1 o'clock. He dressed quickly, put the gun he had found in the barn inside his belt at the back of his trousers, and pulled a jacket over the top. It was very uncomfortable, and he didn't think the police in America would carry such a weapon in such an uncomfortable place. He crept to the top of the landing and down the stairs, only to come face to face with the two men from yesterday. He pulled the gun out of his trouser belt and pointed it straight at one of them. Both men put their hands not exactly in the air but where Martin could see them, and in that calm but unsettling voice, he said, "I have just rung the police. They will be here soon. Shall we sit and wait for them?"

Slowly, they backed away, then quickly turned and ran. Unfortunately, Martin couldn't follow them as his trousers were falling down around his ankles. That definitely didn't happen in any film he had watched. He returned to his bedroom, got dressed properly, shaved, and decided to sleep in the lounge just in case the two men should return.

Chapter Seventeen

Police Sergeant Roy Greisley was sitting on the same small hill amongst the shrubs and saplings that Gibson had occupied, also watching over the old farmhouse. It was now 8:30 in the morning. A very sharp frost had descended in the night, and although he wore the appropriate clothes, it was still bitterly cold. He was crouching down in the vain hope that the occupier would lead him to where the parchments were. He hadn't really thought it through properly, but had to start somewhere. He had no idea about the two men who had broken into the house earlier, but Roy was confident those papers would not be in the house.

Martin had slept fitfully throughout the night, and all sorts of questions were buzzing around his head. Uppermost, he thought he had better check the measurements of the book to ensure they corresponded with the sizes he had given the carpenter, also an idea of the weight, and, as an afterthought, get a load of materials together to put into the second box to act as a decoy. They had to be of a similar weight. Like all times before setting off into the mountain, he made sandwiches and flasks, then also added to his rucksack a tape measure and some digital cooking scales. They were only small but ideal for what he wanted. Before he donned his warmest clothes, he gave Chloe a quick ring. It was her mother's funeral today, and he wanted to cheer her up. He did more than that when he told her that after he removed his gun from his belt to warn the two guys off and tried to look the tough man that he knew he wasn't. His trousers were falling down as soon as the gun was removed because that left the belt loose.

"She couldn't stop laughing," and after wishing her all the best, they said their goodbyes and rang off.

Martin locked up the house, got onto his quad bike, and drove out the rear of his property. There was a narrow gateway with large stone pillars on each side, which the quad only just went through. Closing the gate behind him, he then continued to drive down the old track. This track would have connected all the farms at one time and would have continued into Corwen. It was now a very bumpy, uneven track. The sides of this track were made up mostly of very large lumps of slate. Some of the sides, where the slate still remained after hundreds of years, had thick moss growing. All these walls would have been built when one of the many slate mines was active. One mine, which closed in 1963 and was halfway up the Berwyn Mountain, was a place Martin had promised himself to visit. Not sure if all these old slate walls were for boundary purposes or for keeping sheep and cattle together in the days when these tracks were used for the drovers, who used to take the animals hundreds of miles into cities to be sold and slaughtered for fresh meat.

Greisley heard the quad start up and was on his feet and following him, half running and half walking, which was difficult to achieve when your body is stiff from being cold and crouching in one position. But following the tracks made by the quad on the frosty surface, banking on the assumption he didn't think he would be travelling far, or at least hoped he wasn't.

The two men who had left Martin's farm earlier that morning had only gone as far as the end of the lay-by and were also now kitting up for the cold weather. They retraced their way back towards the farm. When they arrived in the yard, they saw Greisley in the distance. Mistaking him for the owner, they decided to follow but had to quicken their pace to keep up with him.

Martin parked his quad at the bottom where the rocky incline started, and in a totally different direction from when he first came to the area. He got off and started climbing. When he reached the bottom of the steps, he glanced back through the trees. He could just make out a man standing by his quad. Martin had no idea who it was, but thought it might be one of the two men who had accosted him in his kitchen. He decided to continue up the steps, then go over the plateau and down the other side. He wasn't too sure how it panned out or even if you could get down there, but it had to be worth a go, trying to picture the layout in his mind. He thought he should come down the same side but much further over, where an old stone barn stood with part of its roof missing. It was a much longer and far more difficult route, with some very large and difficult rocks to negotiate. You certainly couldn't get up that way, but it was far better to be safe than sorry.

While the policeman was a little way off, he had seen Martin dismount the quad and start to climb the rocks. He ran to catch up and was standing by the quad before trying to follow him up this rocky outcrop and work out where Martin had ascended. What Greisley didn't know was that two men were still following him. They, in turn, were now puzzled if it was the owner of the parchments who was standing by the quad or someone else. They hadn't heard the quad when they left the farmhouse and weren't too sure who owned the vehicle now that they had seen it. The two reprobates were out of breath, trying to keep up this gruelling pace and keeping out of sight as much as possible, but ran forwards to catch him up when they saw him start to scramble amongst the rocks and vegetation above them. Neither of these two men wanted to follow up a mountain, so one took out his gun, aimed it at Greisley's legs, and fired. He only meant to stop him, but no handguns over that distance are very accurate at the best of times. The policeman dropped down and was wedged between two rocks.

The two men, already out of breath, climbed up to where they had shot. It took a few moments to locate him. They did so by the splatter of blood over the rocks. As soon as they saw him, they realised it was a different man they had shot.

"Bugger, what do we do with him? It ain't who we are after."

"He ain't dead. 'Ang on, who the 'ell are you?" one of the two men demanded.

"Roy Greisley," he replied in quite a strained voice. "You just shot me," stating the obvious. "I need an ambulance, and by the pain in my chest, I need it quickly."

"Well, you had better ring for one then. We ain't got time for this," said the other, then turned to his companion. "Nobody will find him here. That bloke we're after must have come on that quad and gone further up. This guy must have been following him, too. We will have to keep climbing."

They climbed for a while but soon realised there was no way they would catch up with anybody, or even if they were going in the right direction. They even argued which way was back to where they had started, then tried to find the man they had shot.

"All these rocks that first appear the same are all different and not helped by all these bloody trees growing out of them," complained one.

Martin had started to descend from the plateau when he heard the gunshot. Were they shooting at him? What did it say about these men, though? Both ruthless and they had guns, and unlike Martin, they also had ammunition, and by the sound of it, not afraid to use them. It appeared they were determined to get their hands on the original documents. What he had to do was be extremely careful and return to the safety of his house, or better still, Evans' house, and get some backup.

After the contorted and difficult descent over the far side of the outcrop, he gradually reached the base after having to drop off one that was over three metres high. Then, onto the track, walking past the old barn. There were many conifers and bare broadleaf trees all along this stretch of track, which wound its way back towards the place he had left his quad. Martin couldn't see any movement of men and hoped they couldn't see him. He was ten feet away from his bike when he felt a whoosh by his head, followed by a loud bang. He knew somebody had fired a gun. Why they wanted him dead, he had no idea. Maybe they didn't appreciate it, but without Martin, nobody could gain entry to the cave and the parchments.

He sprinted to his bike, fired it up. The bike was blown into the air with a loud explosion as it disintegrated beneath him. Martin was thrown some 20 feet away, landing unceremoniously into a ditch — but also now completely deaf.

The ditch was full of dirty, icy water. He started to stumble back towards the old barn, keeping low in the ditch. His head hurt abominably; he could hardly think. Blood was running down his leg, his breathing was now erratic, short, and rasping; even with his lack of medical knowledge, it was not a good sign. There wasn't a part of his body that didn't hurt. But self-preservation is a weird thing and something to do with adrenaline.

Stumbling along, he was now behind a large rock some 150 feet away when he saw the two men arrive from off the outcrop at the destroyed quad bike. Then, to his dismay, a tractor trundled down the track towards them. Eventually, the tractor, along with Evan driving, reached the burnt-out remains with the two men standing next to it.

Although his hearing was returning, Martin couldn't hear what the conversation was about between them. All he wished was that Evan would leave them to it and go back home. There was no way he wanted his friendly neighbour to get mixed up with any shooting.

After a few minutes, Martin was able to hear better and heard Evan say, "This is private land, now bugger off and go back the way you came," and with that, he started up his tractor and turned, going back the way he had come.

As soon as Evan reached his house, he rang the police and told them he was concerned for his neighbour, and that his quad bike had, what looked like to him, been blown up. Also, two suspicious men were standing over it. He then jumped into his Land Rover, deciding to go over to Martin's house after trying to ring him on both his landline and his mobile. Just as he pulled up in front of Martin's house, a van came behind him. It was the man who had made the boxes. They automatically spoke and greeted each other in Welsh. Evan told the carpenter that Martin had disappeared, and he was worried about him.

"Leave the box in the back of the Land Rover. Does he know how much he owes you?"

"Yes, tell him to give me a ring when he shows up," putting the boxes in the back of Evan's vehicle and shooting off.

Evan was puzzled over two boxes. On inspection, they were very well made, with strong straps and padding where they would lie over the carrier's back. He wondered if one was to be a decoy. If it was, it was a good move. He rang his son to see what time he would be arriving.

"Just leaving Stirling Lines in Hereford now. Takes about two and a half hours. Hwyl am y tro."

The two men had no intention of 'buggering off' as that stupid Welsh farmer had said, then carried on looking for Martin. The man who had shot at him had no intention of killing him but wanted to frighten him into handing over these so-called parchments. They had no idea how many or how big they would be, but they never usually had this much problem in getting things they had been ordered to retrieve.

Before any of the local police officers went looking for Martin, one of them rang DI Brown at Cambridge CID. He remembered Martin telling him they were involved. He repeated to Brown what had been told to him by Evan Griffiths.

"From what you have just told me, Constable, Martin Ambrose is in imminent danger of his life. You need to try and locate him as quickly as possible," and told the young Welsh constable the conversation he and Martin had had the day before.

"Would you be so kind as to keep me in the loop?" and gave him his own mobile number, and then added, "I don't want to be a nuisance, but could I come and add my pennyworth in North Wales?"

"It would be good for joint areas to come together. No doubt you know more about this situation than we do. Look forward to having your company and input," and told Brown their postcode and where they were.

"This arsehole must be about here somewhere," said one, as the two men searched the area, looking amongst rocks and undergrowth. They eventually found Martin curled up in the ditch as he lay in freezing water. They pulled him out of the soggy trench, sitting him with his back against a rock.

"Where are these bloody parchments?"

With tears of absolute pain and through gritted, chattering teeth, he told them, "In a cave up that mountain."

"Show us," and started to push him forward, but he fell in a heap. They got one on each side of him and tried dragging him, but it was hopeless.

"How far up is it?"

"Towards the top," he replied with a very croaky voice.

"Let's tie him up and leave him in that barn down there. Then we can go there ourselves. We can always come back and work him over if we can't find what we are looking for."

By the time they reached the barn, Martin had collapsed, and the two men ended up dragging him the last few yards. Not trusting anything to chance, not even a man who looked next to dead, they tied his hands together with electrician's insulating tape, which they always carried for such a situation, and stuffed a piece of old rag in his mouth, which they found lying on the floor. Once they were happy Martin wasn't going to go very far, they set about putting some wooden posts and tin across the opening of the barn, which had obviously been used before for that very purpose. Then they set out in search of these so-called old parchments in a cave at the top of this damned mountain, and hopefully before it got too dark.

Chapter Eighteen

Martin came drifting back to consciousness, thinking his head would explode; the pain was so bad. He could hardly breathe, with something revolting stuck in his mouth. On top of that, his chest felt as if somebody was standing on it and trying to crush it, and by the feel of it, they were winning. He was also soaking wet, extremely cold, and shivering. On the bright side, if there was one, he was out of the rain. Through his muddled brain, he knew he had to do something. The first thing was to try to remove this object from his mouth; it only felt as if it had been pushed into his mouth.

As he was propped into the corner of what he thought might be the old barn, he scraped his face along the rough stone wall. First one way, then, with a lot of pain around his neck, the other way, where the pain was even worse. At the same time, trying to force out the rag with his tongue, it eventually came out. Then he worked up saliva to spit out the small particles left behind. By this time, the exertion had been too much, and with the chronic pain both in his chest and his head, he must have passed out again.

Dafydd, Evan's son and the only other Welshman in

the entire regiment, Gareth Owen, Dafydd's oldest friend, arrived at his father's farm at 3 o'clock in Gareth's Nissan Navara 4x4. Dafydd was a little over 1.7 metres high and of a slight but very muscular build, while Gareth, a little over 1.8, was built like a solid brick wall. Like all those in the SAS, they were both immensely fit, would go for a 10-mile jog with a full backpack of 25 kilos, just as anybody else would go for a stroll in the woods. His mum was delighted to see them both, fussing about, making tea, dishing out cakes and biscuits to sustain them till dinner was served.

It was ten minutes later when Evan burst through the farmhouse door, followed by two policemen, who had seen Evan going into his house. Evan then set about telling the two army friends the entire situation, with the two constables listening in, especially how worried he was when he discovered two suspicious characters standing over Martin's disintegrated quad bike.

So, with no more ado, the two constables climbed into the rear of Gareth's vehicle with Evan leading the way in the Land Rover. They drove out of the farmhouse yard, down the track similar to Martin's track, to what was the old drovers' track where the remains of the quad were. They all got out of their vehicles and inspected the area.

"Definitely an explosion, at a guess, a bullet hit the fuel tank," said Dafydd, stating partially the obvious, but then he was an explosives expert. Then continued, "If Martin was sitting on this, he would be very badly injured or dead. Shall we spread out and look about, see if we can see him?"

They automatically concurred as Evan removed his mobile from his jacket pocket and rang for an ambulance, fearing the worst.

The search was widening, clambering over rocks, up and down the old drovers' path, behind old stone walls, but it was one of the policemen who called everybody over, finding a body jammed between two rocks. Evan rushed over, bent down, expecting the worst. "This isn't Martin, but whoever it is, he looks dead."

"Don't touch anything, we need to tape this area off and get SOCO and the rest of the ensemble to carry out an investigation," said the constable who had just found the body.

"We still need to find Martin, though. This gentleman is dead, hopefully Martin isn't," commented Evan. "Let's spread out and carry on walking towards the old barn." It was some ten minutes later when they were pulling away the corrugated tin sheeting and posts that were lying across the front of the barn.

"This was not left like this!" Evan said as he dismantled this temporary door as quickly as he could. Evan knew there was something amiss as he was getting upset and expecting the worst. Dafydd and Gareth both saw the figure of a man slumped across the corner as soon as they entered, his hands held together with electrician's insulating tape.

They cut the tape from his hands and carefully laid him down.

"He's alive," said Gareth, feeling his pulse. "I take it this is Martin?" he said to Evan, who was standing looking anxious behind the two army lads.

Evan rang his wife to see if the ambulance had arrived.

"We have found Martin, and he is alive, but looks very bad. Gareth is attending to him now. I will send Dafydd back to the farm in the Land Rover. Tell the medics to fit it out with a stretcher and to come down here urgently, they won't get down here with the ambulance, that's for sure."

His son was immediately on his feet, running back towards the Land Rover. He happened to glance up at the rock formation and noticed two people high up the mountain amongst the trees. Ignoring them for the time being, and not wanting them to know he had seen them, he jumped into his father's vehicle and went as fast as he could back towards the farmhouse. Two more police cars had also arrived, both in 4x4s.

Dafydd turned the Land Rover round in the farmyard. The police had obviously been briefed by their colleague about the dead man they had found. Both knew Dafydd and were dropping the back to make it longer, throwing out rolls of wire, posts, and goodness knows what, which included two identical boxes to make room for the stretcher, which was perfect timing as the ambulance turned up just then. They then put in the stretcher, which was hanging over the back slightly, two large bags with medical paraphernalia. One medic jumped in the back, the other in the front. The farmer's son drove back the way he had come as fast as he could without shaking everybody to bits, with the suspension being as hard as it was, followed by the two police vehicles.

Dafydd backed the Land Rover as close to the old barn's entrance as he could. After directing the police to where the dead body was, the medics quickly got out along with their bags and were soon tending to Martin. It was half an hour later when they loaded Martin, who was now strapped onto the stretcher after being stabilised, and onto the back of the Land Rover, apparently only just alive. One medic beside him and one in the front as before, with Evan driving very slowly back towards the farmhouse. Once back to where the ambulance was, they transferred him reverently into the back and gave him gas and air to help him with the pain, then on to the Maelor Hospital in Wrexham.

"When I was just turning off the drover's path to the farm, I saw two men up the mountain. Do you fancy a bit of a recce?" Dafydd asked Gareth when he got back to where they had found Martin. He didn't need to be asked twice. Returning to the scene of the crime, they then walked past the gathering police vehicles and the Scene of Crime Officers, now clad in white scene-of-crime suits. The two friends started to ascend the rocks. They walked this way and that, going ever higher, but didn't find anyone.

"What is this all about?" Gareth asked his friend as they started back down from the large outcrop of rocks that formed part of the base of this part of the mountain.

"I'm not sure, but Dad feels it's very important. He would not have asked us to come otherwise, but there is definitely something worth killing people for, that's for certain.

Dad's a good judge of character and must think a lot of Martin, so for the time being, we will do our best to help where we can. I think they need us badly."

Gareth pulled his Nissan up outside Dafydd's dad's farmhouse, just as his dad came out of the house and jumped in the back with another policeman.

"Drive up to Martin's house, will you, Gareth— Gwion's old place."

They pulled up in front of Martin's back door. Luckily, Martin had given Evan a backdoor key. They were just entering, going into the kitchen, when another car pulled up behind Gareth's Nissan. Two gentlemen got out of the car and also approached the back door.

"My name is Detective Inspector Brown, and this is DI Oakley. We are from Cambridge CID," he said, removing and showing them their warrant cards. "This is Martin Ambrose's house, I assume. Is one of you three gentlemen he?"

Evan introduced them all as he opened Martin's back

door, then nearly broke his neck tripping over a black cat that came flying in. He then went on to tell the two police inspectors exactly what had happened in the last few hours.

"Let me get this straight," said Brown. "Martin's quad bike had been blown up. Mr. Griffiths drove up there after hearing an explosion and saw two men standing over the remains of it. You went back to your farmhouse and, with your son and his friend, decided to search for Martin, then discovered a dead person who wasn't Martin. After you all carried on searching, you found Martin tied up in a barn, almost dead. The paramedics are taken down there in the back of your Land Rover. Martin is treated and brought back to your farmhouse, also in the back of a Land Rover, then into an ambulance and onto the hospital."

"That sounds about right," said Evan, then continued, "Dafydd had seen two men up the mountain before he went to get the medics, but when we had safely got Martin underway, these two," he indicated to the two army friends. "Went looking for these two men up the mountain."

"You two went up a mountain looking for two possibly very dangerous men with guns? Are you mad?" said Brown.

The Welsh policeman who had come with Evan quickly intervened and spoke up.

"I have known Dafydd most of his life. You should be feeling sorry for the two so-called dangerous men. These two are in the SAS."

"What you do and how you do it in North Wales has nothing to do with me. I am also shocked about Mr. Ambrose, and you say another gentleman has been found shot and killed, and you have no idea who that is? This gets worse. However, what I am interested in, though, is what has happened to these so-called ancient parchments. They are apparently of national importance according to some academics."

None of them could help Brown there.

"As far as we know," said Evan, not realising that what they were about to transport to London was so important, "they are still in the same secure place that only Martin seems to know about. Where that is, none of us has got the slightest idea."

"We have one thing in our favour," said Brown. "We have been sitting in our car in this lay-by for half an hour. As it was cold, we sat with the engine and heater on. There is a dash-cam connected, and it would have picked up the two men and their car registration, which was parked in front of us, when they drove off a while ago. Now I don't know if these are the men we are looking for, but it's got to be worth a try. Is there anyone who can upload the memory card?"

"Hang on a second, I will find out," said the local policeman, while he rang the station and spoke in Welsh to somebody on the other end. After a few minutes of talking, he turned to DI Brown.

"Right, go out of the drive, turn left," and gave Brown the rest of the directions to the police station, then added, "Hefin is expecting you. Give him the memory card. He will do a PNC. We will get them before they leave Wales. That's if the car's not stolen and they haven't yet got back into England."

Chapter Nineteen

The two Cambridge detectives drove the short distance into Corwen. The police station was at the far end of the village. It was a fairly new and spacious building that also housed the fire and ambulance emergency services. They were shown into the control room where they handed over the Dash-cam memory card, then were offered and given coffee. Brown asked the officers. "How well do you know the area? Also, do you know Evan Griffiths and Martin Ambrose?"

"The area I know very well," said the older of the two officers. "I have known Evan Griffiths for forty years, Dafydd, his son, since he was born, Martin Ambrose we know nothing about, but if Evan says he's good, then that's OK by me. Here is what your dash-cam registered." They saw the car registration clearly, and then the two men hurriedly got into their car and drove off. He handed the registration number to another policeman, who went off to do what was necessary. It's only 16 miles to the border; they will be well gone by now, I am afraid. What do you want to do?"

"Well, it was worth a try, and time is getting on; we had better get somewhere to stop the night. Any suggestions?"

"Go back towards Llangollen for about five miles, the Berwyn Arms is on the left, you will be OK there, and it's been nice to have met you, albeit briefly."

The two detectives drove back a little dejected, and decided to pop into see Mr. Griffiths farmhouse, grumbling that they had nothing to eat since breakfast, there was no street lighting and then missed the turning to the Griffiths property, so had to turn round and go back, on the plus side there was very little traffic, they were about to knock on the door when it swung open and Gareth stood there, for all intense and purpose he blocked out all the light emitted from the room behind him, neither detective had appreciated the size of the man before, "I wonder if I may have a few words with you all, Gareth stepped back so they could enter into the warm fragrant kitchen.

As soon as they entered, Mrs. Griffiths said, "Don't just stand there letting the cold in, sit down, I will make you a fresh cup of tea, have you eaten anything yet?"

"Er, nothing since breakfast."

"Would you like some lamb stew? I always have plenty on the go when these two are about. It's like feeding the entire regiment."

"That is very kind of you, thank you very much."

While they were eating, the inspector asked them how long they had lived here, just as a conversational way of opening some sort of dialogue. "There have been a

Griffiths here for hundreds of years," said Evan.

Then Mrs. Griffiths added. "We are the fourth generation since Evan's grandfather bought the farm off the Wynn's some 50 years ago, but they have farmed it far longer."

"So you know the area pretty well then?"

"Not much of the area I don't know," replied Evan.

"Do you know of any caves or similar places where these so-called ancient parchments could be kept?"

"There are no caves as far as I know, there are some beautifully carved steps, but they only go to a viewing point, there are slate mines at Moelferna quarry, which was started in 1876 and shut in the 1960s, that's over and above Glyndyfrdwy, not far from here. Martin told me just before everything kicked off that he had something very valuable that needed to be taken to the British Museum, and he had two boxes made with carrying straps to transport them. Martin also asked for my help in shifting them, and we both decided to get help from these two," pointing to the two army lads. "To transport them to the British Museum in London, Martin said they were heavy and in a very difficult place, hence the reason why they are here. He also told me that the less I knew, the safer I would remain, promising to tell me everything once these articles were safely in the museum. That is all any of us know."

"Well, that stew was absolutely delicious, Mrs. Griffiths. We will be back in the morning to have a better look round, we haven't far to go as we will be staying at the Berwyn Arms, I think he said, err, the name of the village completely escaped me," and took their leave.

The two detectives hadn't gone long when there was another knock on the door, and like before, Gareth opened it. He was stunned for a few minutes as an attractive young lady stood there, and she looked in a bit of a state. "Is Mrs. Griffiths in?" she asked nervously.

Again, Gareth stood back to let her in. "I'm Chloe Stone I have been to my mother's funeral earlier to-day and have been also trying to contact Martin all day, I was so worried I have just driven from Cambridge, I went to his house but it's all locked up, do you know what has happened?" she asked sitting down at the table and cradling a cup of tea that had been handed her.

"Have you had anything to eat?" asked Mrs. Griffiths, spooning a bowl of stew and handing it to her without waiting for an answer, making sure she had cutlery. She then told Chloe everything that had happened.

"How is Martin?" asked Chloe apprehensively.

"We rang the Maelor Hospital a while back and they told us 'As well as can be expected,' standard answer, I am afraid."

Just then, Evan came in the door. "Chloe," he exclaimed. "Through all this excitement, I had forgotten about you. I do apologise. I see you have met my son and his friend Gareth, and you have also been fed."

"Please accept my apologies for disturbing you. I

really appreciate the stew. It's delicious, I will be off as soon as I have finished it."

"You will be doing nothing of the sort young lady, you can stay the night in one of the bedrooms, we have plenty," so between the three men they made up a bed in one of the many bedrooms, which was a bit awkward under the circumstances as these three, who were eager to help a women in distress, unfortunately these men were trying to do what Mrs. Griffiths could have done on her own in minutes.

In the morning Chloe went downstairs to a cacophony of noise in the kitchen, it was full of people including two Cambridge detectives, some of the local police were also there, and Mrs. Griffiths serving teas and coffees as if it was a cafe, she spoke in Welsh and English, transferred them both without batting a hair, added to all this mayhem a Collie dog decided he needed some attention from this pretty women who had just wondered in. "Never mind this lot," said Mrs. Griffiths as Chloe stood in the doorway. "Come and sit down, and I will get you some breakfast, bacon, eggs, and toast, and I will brew you a fresh cup of tea. It's nice having a young lady about rather than all these men, most of them oversized." Then, she spoke to the dog in Welsh, and he immediately returned under the enormous kitchen table.

"Ah! Professor Stone," said Brown. "The very person I want to see," he took out his notebook and launched into a tirade of questions.

Evan stepped in. "Give her a break, man, the woman's eating her breakfast."

Looking very sheepish, Brown um'd and ar'd a bit then finished his cup of tea Mrs. Griffiths had given him. After a few minutes, took a deep breath as he looked at his notes. "We are led to believe these parchments, or whatever they are described as, are up a mountain somewhere near here. Would that be correct?"

"Yes, I have been there a couple of times with Martin; they are at the top of a set of stone steps."

"I have been up those steps a few times; the only thing at the top of those steps is a view of the Dee valley," interrupted Evan, which was concurred by his son, then they realised they had interrupted the inspector again.

"There is a fabulous view from up there but when Martin touches the back wall the rock moves to one side revealing a cave, Martin had no idea why it happened until he discovered that he is a direct descendant of Merlin, and before you all scoff, I didn't believe it until he showed me his family tree going back to 700 AD and demonstrated the rock moving, which was after nothing had happened when I touched it."

"I knew there was a reason I liked Martin; he's Welsh." Jumped in Evan again.

Brown ignored this extra tirade, "So you can't open the cave," persisted Brown.

"Nobody can, Martin and I both came to the conclusion that only a descendant of Merlin can, and as

Martin is probably the only remaining relative, he alone can open it." She then added, "I know it sounds a bit sci-fi but what you cannot dismiss is, evidence proved without contradiction when it happens in front of your very eyes, I, like the rest of you in this room, as well as Martin himself, when he first discovered what was happening didn't believe any of it, he never went looking for a cave or anything to do with Merlin, up until quite recently he had no idea about any of this, he just wanted to lead a quiet retirement.

Chapter Twenty

Detective Inspector Brown and Detective Sergeant Oakley entered the Maelor Hospital in Wrexham at 12 o'clock on that same morning. They asked the receptionist, whilst showing their warrant cards, where they would find Martin Ambrose. She indicated the general direction and told them they wouldn't miss the ward as a policeman was sitting outside the door. The corridors were, if anything, a little sad-looking but were scrupulously clean, and very few people were about. "These corridors go on forever," commented Oakley as they turned another corner.

Eventually they turned into the ward and then into the private section where Martin was recovering, with the policeman sitting on a chair looking very bored outside, as soon as he saw the two police officers walking towards him, he removed his note book from his breast pocket, at the same time as the two Cambridge officers, removed their warrant cards for him to make a note of their names, along with the time they arrived. "He has just come round, sir," the constable said as they entered the ward.

A nurse was administering some clinical ministrations, without looking up at the two new arrivals, continued writing her notes down onto a clipboard, then hung it back on the end of the bed. "He came round about an hour ago, although he is still very groggy," she said, barely looking at them as she walked out the door.

The inspector pulled up a hard chair next to the bed and sat on it. "We meet at last, Mr. Ambrose. I'm Detective Inspector Brown. We think we have pieced together what has happened. Is there anything you can tell us to help us capture these men?"

"I don't think," Martin started feeling and sounding very shaky, pointing to a glass of water on a cupboard on the opposite side from where Brown was sitting. Brown went round, picked it up, and realised he would have to administer the drink to his mouth.

"You were saying, sir."

"One held a gun in his left hand and limped slightly; I think they were both from London by their accents."

Just then, a doctor walked into the room. "Don't tire him; we are still unsure of his head injuries."

"How bad are his injuries?"

"Apart from his lungs being damaged through a broken rib, a very badly twisted leg, and a Colles' fracture, and many quite bad cuts, which have all been treated as far as it goes, we await now to see how his head injuries are, then we can release him if everything is OK. Should be in about a week."

As there was nothing else the two detectives could do or ask, they left and returned to the Berwyn Arms in a place called Glyndyfrdwy, which neither policeman would even try to pronounce. The manager stopped them when they entered. "Did you say you two were detectives?"

"Yes, from Cambridge, why?"

"Well, a man booked in a few days ago, he went out and hasn't returned, I'm sure he said he was also from Cambridge."

"Could we see his room?"

"Yes, follow me," they went up the old stairs, past the rooms the detectives were occupying, along a corridor, and through a doorway. "This is the oldest part of the building, reputedly 14th century; it's in here," and beckoned them in.

It was an odd shaped room, consequently none of the furniture fitted properly, there was a suitcase on the floor, the lid was down but not locked, clothes neatly laid out on the bed, under them was a wallet, Brown opened it to discover the usual credit cards, a library card, a drivers licence, £100 in cash and something he wasn't expecting, a police warrant card, he studied the two pictures, one on the driving licence and one on the warrant card, turned them both towards his sergeant, "Would you say these two pictures are of the same man, I am wondering if it's of the gentleman found dead?"

Oakley studied them for a minute, "Yes, I would, and a good assumption as he only went missing very recently."

They immediately put blue surgical gloves on and searched the rest of the room. They discovered copies of notes made by Professor Stone, which were in the bottom drawer of the bedside cupboard. After a quick glance over them, he turned to Oakley. "Get this lot bagged up, we will inform the local lads to do a thorough search, I think we will go over to Martin Ambrose's house and have a nosey around there, before going to the place where this gentleman was killed, what he was doing here and why, is a bit of a mystery though."

They drove the relatively short distance to Martin's house. Professor Stone was there, standing in the doorway, having been given a key by Evan, and she invited the two detectives in. "Coffee?" she asked.

"That would be nice, we have not long left, Mr. Ambrose, he seems to be recovering well."

"I am delighted to hear that, they tell you nothing over the phone I will go over to the hospital later, I feel partly responsible for his injuries, had I listened to Martin in the first place none of this would have happened, I was so excited about the material he had shown me at the beginning, I convinced him to show me more."

"Are these Mr. Ambrose's family tree, err, documents, or whatever they are called?" he asked, looking down onto the dining room table top.

"Yes, I have just been putting them all back in order, ready to put them back in that box, so don't mess them up."

Brown picked up a few sheets, looking at the dates and names. These are quite unbelievable. I take it they are genuine?"

"Yes, they are, he has probably one of the finest lineage and ancestry trees in Britain."

"I thought I would go up this mountain and look for myself. Would you be so kind as to show me the way?"

"You will need better footwear than you are wearing now, and a warmer coat would be beneficial; it will be very cold up there."

After a few pleasantries, they finished their coffee, returned to their car, and decided not to go climbing up any mountain. "Next," he said to his sergeant as they started it up. "The Griffiths."

"She is too pretty and too young to be a professor," remarked Oakley.

"She has more brains and far more respect than either of us put together, that is for sure, if what all her colleagues say about her," and then continued more to himself than to Oakley. 'If Ambrose is a direct descendant of Merlin, and it looks highly probable looking at his family tree, it's the reason why the professor meant when she said, only Martin can open the cave, and probably why it's remained hidden for over 1200 years, and he only discovered it by accident."

"Yes, but I am struggling to get my head round this 'magic' thing," he said the word as if it was a word that shouldn't exist. "A bloody great stone moves by placing a hand on it, nah! I don't believe it."

"That is as may be," retorted Brown. "Why would they make it up, and knowing or owning what he does, look where it's got him?"

By this time, they had arrived at the Griffiths' farmhouse. Oakley knocked on the door, and it was opened by Dafydd, who stepped back to let the two policemen in. "Do you happen to know if the SOCOs have finished yet?"

"Shouldn't think so, judging by all the vehicles going up there, I didn't know Wales had so many people working for the police."

"Would it be too much trouble for one of you to take me up there? I have just found out who I think the dead man is; it may be helpful to the SOCOs to be given that bit of information."

"Anybody we would know?"

"Doubtful, he was a policeman, and like us, also from Cambridge."

Without being asked anything else, Dafydd said. "Come on, then, with me." They piled into the Land Rover and proceeded to drive along the now even muddier and bumpier track, which seemed to be getting worse by every passing vehicle, not being helped by this persistent rain.

They arrived at the bottom of the outcrop. DI Brown saw one of the detectives from yesterday; he got out of the Land Rover, intending to go across to speak to him, but sank up to his ankles in mud. "Bugger," he raised his voice slightly. "Could I have a word with you, please?" he beckoned one of the SOCOs over to him.

"You should have put on Wellington boots," he said, stating the obvious in a slightly sarcastic way, but coming over towards the Land Rover and the Cambridge detectives.

"I have written down all the details of the man whom I think was killed," handing the Welsh inspector a sheet of paper. "For your information, he was one of ours, inasmuch as a police officer, and he was staying at the Berwyn Arms. I removed some papers from the scene that will help my side of the inquiry. I will get them photocopied and let you have a copy of them," waving a plastic wallet. "I have also spoken to your men at Corwen station to carry out a detailed search. I hope that will save you a bit of time," he added sarcastically. "Bye for now." With that, Brown got back into the vehicle, complete with muddy shoes, turned to Dafydd, calling him David, and asked if he would drive him back.

"That's my name in English, did you know, spelled totally different though." They pulled up at the farmhouse to see Chloe also pulling up.

I thought you would like to go and see for yourself, both the terrain and difficulty from where the old parchments are, to getting them down the mountain, and before you take them on to the British Museum. I know you know the area well, but I think Martin would very much appreciate it," said Chloe, hoping that Dafydd would agree. Then, seeing the inspector getting out of the Land Rover, said. "Do you want to come?"

"I will give it a miss, as you quite rightly pointed out, I don't have the appropriate footwear and clothing," said the inspector.

"I will get some decent clothes on then; I expect Gareth will want to come," said the man who was twice as wide as she was.

Chapter Twenty-One

Stanley Gibson was not happy when a man turned up unannounced at his home, informing him there was far more opposition than they were led to believe. "So, tell me again, how many people know about these bloody so-called parchment things?"

"As far as I know, the only people who know about the parchments, other than ourselves, are Professor Stone and the owner of them, I now think his name is Martin Ambrose. Oh! and possibly the police, but they won't be running around after some old pieces of paper."

"Wrong, we shot one man who is probably now dead, we have blown another up, but later discovered it may have been this Martin Ambrose, we tried to get him to show us where the parchments are kept, but we couldn't get him to move very far, we tied him up and left him in an old barn so we could equip ourselves better, but not before we tried to find a so called cave at the top of a mountain. Then, while we were looking, more people arrived; we didn't hang about but came back here to have a quiet word with you."

Gibson was horrified to learn the ruthlessness of these men, but asked all the same. "So you haven't yet managed to secure the goods?" he only just managed.

"We have spent a considerable amount of time and money so far, I am here to renegotiate how much you are prepared to pay us to continue, now you said these goods could be worth in excess of one million pounds, how much excess would that be, and how much is it worth to you for me, not putting a bullet through your head now."

Gibson was quiet for some time before answering, "OK, what about 50 -50 split on the sale price, I really have no idea of how much they would be worth, I have to find a buyer then I have to negotiate the price, I can't put it into auction now can I, especially if you have gone round shooting everybody to get the bloody things."

The man stood up, removed his gun from inside his jacket pocket, and pointed it straight at Gibson, "I think I will kill you now and cut our losses."

"What else do you want me to do? I don't have any idea of the value of the bloody things. I wish I hadn't got into it. What if I give you 75% of what I get for them?"

"That sounds better, but if you try to cheat us, I will put a bullet straight through that skull of yours," and with that, he left Gibson in a state of deep despair.

******

DI Brown and Sergeant Garry Allsop, who was a short, stocky man with more brawn than brains, although once a year he would have a flash of brilliance, unfortunately, the last one was only six months ago, and Brown wasn't expecting any flashes any time soon. They both went along to Roy Greasley's house back in Cambridge, they also took with them WPC Shirley Draycote as a family liaison officer, Brown would have preferred her to almost any other detective, she was intelligent, perceptive, quick witted and above all, she showed common sense, but best of all she was also pleasing to the eyes, Brown had been encouraging her to sit her sergeants exam which she was doing next week.

They arrived at Greasley's house. The moment Mrs. Greasley opened the door, she knew something was wrong. She was small, neat with a plain face and small brown button eyes, which were now peering at them in a pleading sort of way. "Can we come in, Mrs. Greasley? I am very sorry, but we have some very sad news to impart," Brown put on his most placatory voice and outward demeanour.

"Oh dear! Is it something to do with Roy?" turning and walking into the lounge with the three detectives following.

"There is no easy way to tell you, but your husband has been found dead in a place called Bonwm near a place called Corwen. I am extremely sorry for your loss."

WPC Draycote made her a cup of sweet tea, while they all sat down in very comfortable, chintz-covered chairs in the lounge. When the tears had subsided a little, DI Brown asked. "Do you know why Roy happened to be in the Corwen area of North Wales?"

Between the snuffles and nose blowing. "Is that

Snowdonia?" she asked with tears still rolling down her cheeks. "Because that was where he said he was going."

"Not really Snowdonia, but close to it and a beautiful place just the same."

"Roy just said he was going walking for a couple of days in Snowdonia, I don't think he had been there before, he used to go off for a couple of days at least once a year, but never at this time, not in the dead of winter. Quite honestly, I was glad to be rid of him for a while so the two girls and I would get a bit of peace and quiet," she responded with tears welling up in her eyes again. "How did he die?"

"We are not too sure, but we think he was shot. I wish there was an easier way of telling you that," he let that bit of information hang in the air for a few seconds before asking. "Did he have anything on his agenda other than going for walks, do you know?"

"No, he was a deeply religious man, as you probably know, maybe he wanted to see what the churches were like, I really don't know."

Brown didn't know he was religious; in fact, he didn't know him at all, but that last comment started to make him think about some of the disclosures in those papers. Brown asked. "Do you know if he had brought any papers home with him, or did he speak about any ancient manuscripts that he had come across during his normal working day?"

"No, he never said anything about his work, he kept

his work and family life very much separate, but he did bring some papers home a few nights ago but they weren't old, just A4 copy paper, they had a lot of double-dutch mysterious writing on though, I only know that, because I found one of the sheets in the waste paper bin, I will go and retrieve it if you like, I put it in the recycling bin." She went out of the room and into the rear of the property, returning after a few minutes, trying to straighten the single sheet out. "Here it is, it's a bit crumpled, I'm afraid. He brought home a few sheets like this. I thought they had come from his church, where he is a lay preacher; he must have discarded this one, he did spend some time studying them all on the dining room table."

As soon as the detectives saw the sheet of paper, they knew it was something to do with the old manuscripts, but why Greasley had taken a trip to North Wales without telling anybody they didn't yet know, Brown had a feeling whatever it was, he was killed either for the information on the sheets of paper, or what the pieces portended to be, which another person thought he had, then had tried to track the originals down.

They asked Mrs. Greasley some further questions, but it was clear she wasn't able to enlighten them any further; she had been kept in the dark, just as much as Greasley had not shared the information he knew with the inspectors, or to anybody else, for that matter. Mrs. Greasley told them she didn't want or need any help from

Shirley, the young WPC, when they asked her, so the three detectives returned to their car and started the journey back to the police station.

It was the first time that the WPC had seen any of the papers; she was now studying this single sheet while sitting on the back seat of their car. "What do you make of it?" asked Brown, seeing in the rear-view mirror what she was doing.

"Well, it's obviously been copied out and then translated by another hand. It looks like a list of cures, or treatments for ailments, they seem very archaic and weird to me, like some sort of medieval treatment, and looking down the sheet, pretty revolting too."

"You would be spot on with that riposte, I believe that sheet was left out of the pile because it was for ailments, the other papers, copied at the same time with the translated words above each word are apparently, and according to some professors and other academics, ground shattering, they were copied from some ancient manuscripts that were over 1200 years old, our sergeant Greasley had obviously photocopied all the sheets, when they had been stolen from a professor Stone who was working on them, by none other than the Bursar at a university where she worked. Now, Greasley was murdered either for (a) the knowledge they contained or (b) trying to obtain the originals and got in the way of somebody else, who also wanted them, possibly for gain as they are worth a lot of money." He let that hang in the air for a few seconds, then continued. "Which brings the idea of killing for these parchments very disturbing."

"Did these papers have religious connotations?" enquired the WPC, trying to think of something intelligent to add to the conversation.

"I know nothing about religion, but I am told by these same so-called academics that what the owners of these parchments have unearthed is ground-shattering. Apparently Offa's dyke wasn't built by Offa, and wasn't built to divide England and Wales but had a much more sinister edge to it, there are many aspects in the papers I have seen, which I have to admit, I am ignorant about, religion being one of them, and yes Shirley, there is much of it that has religious connotations that to a religious person would find very offensive, that I am quite certain about."

"Maybe, just maybe," she went on. "Sergeant Greasley wanted to obtain the original documents to destroy them, because in his mind they were defamatory against his beliefs, that's if what Mrs. Greasley say's about her husband being deeply into religion, and when he saw the papers, it sparked something off, but for him to be in North Wales, around the same time as these papers are unearthed, is to my mind far too much of a coincidence, how many papers are there in total?"

"We have seen about ten, all similar to this one and all from different parts of the book they took them out apparently, but according to the owner there are many more, how many more I don't know, the chap who owns them, his name by-the-way is Martin Ambrose, has said they are very well hidden, in fact where they are is where they were written, and they have been there for over 1200 years, or so I am led to believe."

"Looking at this sheet, I recognise the odd Latin word. Are they all as difficult to read as this?" asked Shirley, fascinated by what she was reading.

"Apparently yes, I have been told the scripts are mainly Latin, but also Old English, French and an assortment of goodness knows what else, that is why there are two different hands of writing, one where they copied off the original, then the second when they had help to translate, even then there are gaps which cannot be deciphered, which some doctor of languages informed me, there probably is no direct translation known."

Chapter Twenty-Two

Inspector Brown and Sergeant Oakley went out to have a word with Mr Stanley Gibson at his home. They knocked purposefully on the Oak door, and it was opened by a cautious Gibson, who looked none too fresh; he certainly hadn't shaved for a few days, and the clothes he wore were the same ones he had on when interviewed at the station.

"Good morning, Mr. Gibson. I need to ask you a few questions, sir. Can we come in, please?" They pushed their way in anyway, showing their warrant cards at the same time.

"Have I got a choice?" he answered, leading the way into a very untidy, quite smelly lounge.

"Not really, sir, I thought you might like to tell me why, first you got Stibbins to follow Professor Stone, then denied it, then went over to North Wales yourself, smashed a double-glazed window to steal copies of these parchments after cutting the professor's bag to gain access to them. You must have known we would know it was you. I believe you work as a Bursar for a University; personally, I would have thought you might just have had enough brains to have worked all this out. But tell me,

Mr. Gibson, what exactly do you do as a Bursar?"

"I manage the non-academic aspects of a university, primarily focusing on its finances and business operations, and am also responsible for managing student, faculty, and staff accounts, handling accounts receivable and payable, preparing financial reports and appraisals, and also have an input in helping with budget creation and strategic financial goals. Also, help ensure the smooth running of all the university's operations," saying all this without a blink of an eye.

"And you are now also partly responsible for the death of a policeman and seriously injuring another person, what do you say about that?"

Gibson was getting out of his seat to start protesting and possibly shouting at the two policemen who were calmly talking like people at a garden party. But he was pushed back down into his chair by the much bigger and stronger Sergeant Oakley, but that didn't stop Gibson's verbal retaliation. "You can't accuse me of anything, I told you before, my main objective was to see if University funds were being wasted, I only went to Wales to try and deal with the owner of these so-called papers, they could be a hoax for all I was aware," responding forcefully.

So calmly Brown asked. "Why did you then get others to try their far more dangerous hand to do your bidding? We don't think it's a coincidence that two men turn up within a couple of days at Mr. Ambrose's house demanding the parchments. Then they were seen again standing over a blown-up quad bike and yet again on the mountain where we believe these artefacts are kept."

"That has got nothing to do with me."

"I think it has everything to do with you, so I am arresting you for encouraging others or commissioning others to carry out the act of theft, which consequently led to the death of an officer of the law. You do not have to say anything. But it may harm your defence if you do not mention when questioned something that you later rely on in court. Anything you do say may be given in evidence. Do you understand?

While Gibson was shouting abuse at the two officers, Oakley spun him round and put the handcuffs on. A squad car was waiting outside his house to take Mr. Gibson to the police station.

"Now, Sergeant, we need a bit more evidence. If he got others to do the persuading, then it makes sense that Gibson would have to pay them. I doubt if he would have that number in readies, so look for his banking books as well as anything appertaining to these bloody parchment things, as he has now been arrested and cautioned, we don't need a search warrant."

They opened all the drawers in the desk in his study and found an enormous amount of betting slips along with a small book, and by the look of it, he kept a record of everything he paid and received; it was probably a habit from his years of being a Bursar, but it looked as if he lost far more than he won. "Why would anybody keep a record of all those losses?"

"He has no wife to check up on him; I don't suppose it matters."

Just at that moment, Oakley shouted to the inspector after they both continued searching for missing bank books. "Well, well, well," said the sergeant. "He has very recently withdrawn £500 and £5000."

"The £500 would have been for Stibbins, the £5000 would have been for these others, that I would have thought wasn't enough for these types of villains, I bet there was a percentage of the merchandise worth to consider, the trouble is we don't know who the others were, and they are still on the loose sergeant, We will have another good look round and then go and interview our university Bursar."

The day had got colder, and by the looks of the clouds, the inspector thought snow was imminent. After grabbing some coffee, they went to interview room two, where Gibson was sitting quietly at the table that was bolted to the floor, with an empty polystyrene cup in front of him. They had a word with the desk sergeant, who had checked all his details beforehand. "I see you have had a drink. Would you like another?"

"No, let's get this over and done with. I need to get home."

"Now, before I turn on the tape recording, I just want to say, you have declined a solicitor. Personally, I think you should have one; these are very serious offences you have committed.”

“Just do your worst, I have done nothing wrong, I hope you locked my house up.”

“No, sir, there is a policeman guarding the entrance at this moment. Shall we proceed?” With no more ado, the inspector switched on the recorder. “My name is Detective Inspector Brown.”

“I am Detective Sergeant Oakley. Would you please tell us your full name and address, sir?” Gibson answered with more of a muffled growl than anything, the sergeant went on. “So, you paid Mr Stibbins £500, what was that for?”

“To find the address where the old parchments are.”

“And he obviously furnished you with that address. Is that your normal way of dealing with this type of merchandise, to break in and take the copies as you couldn’t find the originals?”

“The window was already smashed.”

They would check for fingerprints on any stone, but in this weather, he would have been wearing gloves. “Moving on, you then paid out a further £5000, what was that for?”

A little surprise, the police knew how much he had paid these other people. “Stibbins gave me a telephone number as he said they were good at negotiating for certain objects; I had no idea they would kill people for it.”

"What would you have expected for that kind of money then?"

"Not to kill anybody he repeated, but to get a monetary deal and maybe set some sort of dialogue going."

The questions went on, repeated many times, but nothing else was forthcoming, so they let him stew in the cells for a few hours.

Chapter Twenty-Three

Martin was eventually discharged from the hospital after two weeks. He was still having some trouble breathing, and his ribs were still painful. The pain from the Colles fracture on his wrist was mainly controlled by tablets; it didn't hurt that much, more annoying than anything else. Chloe had come to take him home, bringing in a clean set of clothes into the hospital, so as soon as he had got himself dressed, the nursing staff insisted that he be wheeled out in a wheelchair, and Chloe drove back to his farmhouse.

Once back in the fold of his own surrounding's it felt oddly strange, he was also feeling very vulnerable, with Chloe's help he packed a load of clothes into a holdall, and asked her if she would drive him down, first to the Griffiths's, so he could thank them for their care in getting him to the hospital, then he would go on to the Berwyn arms and stay there until the parchments were safely in the British Museum. Chloe would then go back to Cambridge. They arrived at Evan's farmhouse just as Evan drew up in his tractor. He was genuinely pleased to see Martin and ushered them both through the door. The collie dog was even more pleased to see his newfound friends. As soon as Bronwyn (as Mrs. Griffiths insisted that she be called) saw Martin, she gave him a big hug, but did not realise that it was painful for him. "Come and sit down, I don't suppose you have had a decent meal for weeks, you can stop for dinner, roast lamb with all the trimmings, it will be ready in about half an hour."

"That's very kind of you. I only came to thank you all for everything you have done for me. I seem to have ingratiated myself with you far too much already."

"Nonsense," said Evan. "I have not had so much fun in years, Dafydd has told us to give him a ring, when you want that book or whatever it is taking to the British museum, as far as they know there is nothing happening with the regiment at the moment at the camp, your two boxes the carpenter made for you are in our barn, and you had a delivery of a brand-new Quad by-the-way. Oh! And lastly, all the police have now gone."

"That's great; I must ring the carpenter and get his money to him. I was just going down to the Berwyn Arms to book in until all this problem dies down. The sooner we get it over and done with, the better I will feel."

"You are not going anywhere, both you and Chloe can stay here if you want, after dinner we will ring Dafydd up, to organise when we can carry out your original assignment, whatever we do, the police have insisted they know all the details, which includes when you decide to take the book to London, after all this trouble there needs to be a proper plan in place. Now then, bring your things with you, Evan and I will show you your room, and Chloe can get her things from your house after dinner.

"As much as I would like to stop," said Chloe, "I have a meeting at the university tomorrow that I will not be able to avoid, I just hope nobody reveals my dealings with Martin and Merlin, trouble is everybody seems to want to know, those papers have started a chain reaction, and least of all I do not want any dealings with that odious little man Stanley Gibson, he should be sacked.

So, it was on a very cold, bleak, overcast day with a promise of more rain if not snow, that following Monday morning, nearly a week after leaving the hospital, Dafydd, Gareth, and Martin made their way up the now still very rutted and muddy track towards the outcrop in Gareth's 4 x 4. The police, both in Corwen and Cambridge, had been informed they were taking the book to the museum today, the British Museum had been notified by Chloe, and as a back-up, further SAS personnel had been asked to stand by. Like all army manoeuvres both the timing and contingencies had been worked out, there was one word of warning, more of a fly in the ointment, the Bursar had been released from the police station, and was at the meeting which Chloe had attended, through some innocent banter between the professors he would have found out that the removal of the parchments was imminent, but thankfully not the exact day.

The three men were all suitably attired against the weather and the climb. They drove to the end of the track and climbed out of Gareth's 4 x 4, having the benefits of army walky-talkies in their tantalus jackets, wired to mouth and ear pieces. Both the army lads had the purpose-made empty boxes strapped to their backs, which Martin had had made. Martin led the way, but soon it became obvious he was now out of condition. However, he wasn't going to let anything stop him. It was when they reached the bottom of the steps that Gareth, who was bringing up the rear, said to Dafydd through their headpieces, "I have a feeling we are being watched."

Dafydd didn't need to ask his friend twice, and would take heed of anything that Gareth said like that. He turned to Martin and relayed the message. Martin indicated to keep going to the top of the steps. By the time Martin had climbed the forty-odd steps, he was really struggling to breathe as much as anything. Once at the top, Martin asked what they should do because we are here."

Both the army lads looked around but couldn't detect any cave or opening, but accepted that something strange was in the offing. "We carry on going over the top of these immediate rocks as if we are not yet at our destination," replied Dafydd, I shouldn't think anybody can see us this far or up here, but let's not take any chances."

Once over the top and behind more of the huge rock

formations that Dafydd knew were up there. "We are out of anybody's line of sight, especially from all sides," claimed Dafydd. He was now getting a bit concerned over Martin's health; he was looking very pale and his breathing very shallow. "Are you okay? You look totally knackered, mate. Tell you what," he dug into one of the many pockets in his jacket and gave Martin two paracetamol tablets, and then fished out a bottle of water from another pocket. "Take these, they should help."

"Do you carry everything with you?"

"Pretty much," and removed a telescope, yet out of another pocket, and was looking around him, now lying down next to his friend, who also had a telescope, while Martin was slumped back against a rock.

"Is that a man up that BT pole?" asked Gareth.

"It sure is, he is probably radioing his colleagues telling them where we are," he dialled the number on his mobile to the local police station to get somebody to check them out. "That should sort them out."

"What I want you to do, Martin, is to stay hidden behind those gorse bushes and rocks, just over there," he said, pointing. "We will come and retrieve you when it's all clear," they also removed the boxes from their backs and left them with him before disappearing. Martin picked up the boxes and moved away from the immediate area, and more or less buried himself in the prickly bushes and between the rocks. The cold wind up here seemed to go right through you. It wasn't long before they returned. "We have had a good look and listened to everything all around. Now we know they are determined to get these parchments, but we either carry on or leave it another day, it's your call, Martin, what do you want to do?"

"Everything is in place, the police know, the SAS know, and the museum is expecting us. Let's crack on and get it done." With that, they descended from the top where they were, with Martin in a lot more pain than he would have liked. Martin placed his hand on the rock and just as before, it quietly but not silently, the whole rock face moved to one side. The two army lads stood in absolute bewilderment. It took them a few moments to gather their wits together, shaking their heads, thinking, 'We thought we had seen everything.' This was the last thing they expected.

They followed Martin into the cave, with their torches switched on, and had a quick glance around. Laid the first box next to all these parchments, and between the two army lads, they carefully and reverently lifted the whole of this pile of old parchments snugly inside. Although Martin never did get to measure the book, it fitted beautifully, then sealing it in with foam so it doesn't move about, and sealing the entire box with Velcro straps. They then placed the other box onto the table and went about filling it with anything to make up a similar weight, wedging it all in the box with more foam brought for the job. Martin marked the box with the book with a small white X, with the large Velcro straps across to keep everything together. The two army lads hoisted the boxes onto their backs, departing out of the cave slightly unceremoniously.

The book that had been lying in one position for over 1200 years was now on the move. "They look terribly heavy and uncomfortable. Are you both OK?" asked Martin, a little concerned.

"I have had more comfortable things on my back, but they aren't overly heavy," was the immediate reply, and the little group started out down the steps. They had descended about a dozen steps when Dafydd turned and asked Martin who was at the back and bringing up at the rear of the group. "How do you shut the cave?"

"I don't, it just shuts on its own accord."

"That's really weird." Just at that moment, the ground shuddered slightly. "That is extremely weird," Dafydd repeated.

Chapter Twenty-Four

Dafydd was making sure Martin was OK and not rushing, so these two were descending the steps far more slower than Gareth. Gareth had reached the bottom of the steps a few minutes ahead of the other two. He was about to jump from one large rock to another when something hit his legs so hard, he fell back and smashed his head on the rock he had just leapt from. One of the two men they thought had left the area then smashed another piece of a branch down onto his head, rendering him totally unconscious. As quickly as they could, but struggled to unstrap the box from his back. This guy was no lightweight, but between them, they managed, one of them put it on his back, and they were off, and as quickly as they could through the trees and rocks, as they knew Martin and another man were following.

Dafydd heard a quad bike start up, only to find his friend jammed between two rocks and unconscious; there was blood seeping out of his head. He scrambled over to him, shouting to Martin to ring for help. Martin rang Inspector Brown, thinking he would get things moving faster than he could. "Tell them to bring the ambulance to the farm and bring everything in Evan's land rover as before, the two crooks have made off on my new Quad, and one of the boxes, probably aiming back towards my farmhouse and onto the road there." Dafydd was pulling his 18 stone of muscle dead weight and best friend into a better position, but it was difficult as he was jammed between the rocks, blood was running down his face, but he was at least breathing.

DI Brown rang the Corwen police up after ringing the ambulance service, who said they would be there in a few minutes; an ambulance crew was only in Corwen. Brown was staggered how quickly they organised things, the Welsh police told him that the road blocks would be in-place in minutes as they were already set-up should the need arise, he went on to say the main A5 would be blocked from Llangollen to Druids corner one way, and the road to Ruthin would also be blocked at Fwyddelwern, and Chirk police would be on the move to block the A5 back into England. Unfortunately, Brown didn't understand one word, but got the gist that all roads were being blocked.

The man who had been up the telegraph pole and had been acting as look out, had picked the two others up from the quad which was now back at Martins house, they then drove their car out of his drive, having anticipated road blocks being put up on all the main roads, they had devised a way out by going a short distance down the A5 and turning left at Llidiart-y-parc. Speed was very dangerous on these narrow twisty roads, but to them speed was everything, crossing the river Dee over the old bridge, then raced on through Carrog village, continuing up and over the Llantysillio mountain and onto the village of Bryneglwys, where they crossed over the Chester road and staying on these very narrow roads towards Rhyd-y-mendwy, the men had worked out which road to take, but hadn't a clue how to pronounce any of the village names. Unfortunately, they were then stuck behind a tractor. They tried blasting him with their horn, but to no avail. The driver couldn't hear them. There was nothing they could do but lose precious time. Once the tractor eventually turned off into a farmyard, they then did something which everybody seems to do when they have been stuck behind a slow-moving vehicle; they put their foot down and went even faster than before.

Unfortunately for the three thieves, somebody was travelling towards them, in the opposite direction; consequently, the inevitable happened. The noise made as the two cars embedded themselves into each other was deafening.

The family car, in which the couple had been making their way to take their new offspring to meet his grandparents for the first time, was hit with such a force that all three occupants were killed instantly. The car with the three thieves who had been travelling at breakneck speeds had suffered not quite so badly. The driver who had swerved slightly had taken the full force of the impact and was dead. So hard had the crash been that the engine was partly embedded in his waist. The passenger, although not dead, was seriously injured. The man in the back however, although very shaken-up was awake, he looked about him dazed in the now total silence, he certainly couldn't stay there and managed to get out of the rear door by painfully kicking it open, then with difficulty opened the boot of the car, removed the box and strapped it to his back, looking all about him to see if he could find a way to get over one of the hedges that were both sides of the road, he stumbled rather than walked back along the road 100 metres to a gate, there was no way to get by the two vehicles, they were totally jammed across the track, and would remain there for some time until somebody came across them, even then it would take some clever dismantling to release them, made worse as now it was miles from any inhabited establishment.

The only one left to walk properly, hoisted the box better on his back and crossed diagonally across one field, going through another gate with mud six inches deep, then another field before joining the B5429, every step he took was agonising, the weight of the box on his back didn't help, the one thing that kept him going was, he was the only one left to reap the rewards of possibly a million pounds. It wasn't long before he came across a public house with a few cars in the car park, he selected an old Volvo, its driver had obligingly left it unlocked. He placed the heavy box in the boot of the car. And hotwired it to short out and start the engine. Cautiously at first, he drove out of the car park and continued his journey along the A55 towards Chester, and all the way to the M6. He stopped at Keele services, parking the Volvo amongst all other cars, put the seat down, and went to sleep. He was totally exhausted, as well as aching all over.

Gareth was still out cold when the paramedics and police arrived some 20 minutes after Martin had called Inspector Brown, which under the circumstances was unbelievably quick. After their initial assessment, they decided to lift him to flatter ground. They slipped three blankets underneath him, and it took six men to lift him into a better position. They then transferred him onto a stretcher; thankfully stretchers are very cleverly designed for all patient sizes. Once the neck and leg braces were in position, they negotiated him into the back of Evan's land rover, part of his legs and the back of the stretcher protruding out the back, with the land rover well down on its suspension at the rear, they drove him gently back to the farmhouse, and then into the ambulance, there they made sure he was plugged into all the monitors, then the ambulance went onto Wrexham Maelor hospital in exactly the same way as Martin had gone, weeks before.

Dafydd and Martin followed behind the Land Rover to the farmhouse in Gareth's 4 x 4, having put the box into the back. "This is now getting out of hand," commented Martin to Dafydd, Gareth's best friend, who was very quiet. "Nothing is worth this amount of trouble. I think we call the whole thing off."

"No way, man, Gareth would be horrified. The crooks think they have the goods, we know they haven't got the right box. We keep going, there is no way Gareth would accept anything other than finishing what we started."

Bronwyn quickly made up flasks of coffee and sandwiches along with crisps and biscuits to eat on the journey to London, Martin rang Chloe to tell her to meet them at Toddington services on the M1, but would later ring with an estimated time of arrival, Dafydd rang Stirling Lines, the headquarters of the SAS, to give them an update and tell them what had happened to Gareth, they were ready with a helicopter if it was needed. The precious cargo still in the back of Gareth's vehicle was now covered by a secure top, also being secured down with straps, on hooks designed for this very purpose, so that it couldn't move about. Once all were ready, Martin and Dafydd then set off to Wrexham hospital, where they needed to see how Gareth was, before they continued their journey to London. "I hope Gareth is OK," said Martin in a sombre, quiet voice. "Especially as they took the false box."

"He will be fine; I think that was a very good move to have two identical boxes like that."

They pulled into Sainsbury's petrol station on the outskirts of Wrexham, which was only round the corner from the Maelor Hospital. Once filled with fuel, they drove out and pulled up outside the hospital entrance. "You stay in the car and push on the horn if anybody approaches you."

Dafydd ran in and asked the receptionist where Gareth was. "Oh," she said, looking at her computer screen. "He hasn't been admitted yet; you would be better off going around to the emergency entrance. He will still be there waiting to be assessed." She told him the quickest way would be to follow the buildings around the outside. "You can't miss it." Dafydd jumped back into the Nissan and drove around to where all the ambulances were parked outside the emergency entrance.

Walking into the assessment area only to find his oversized mate standing there, arguing to be released. "I was only having a kip," he argued. Luckily, they were talking in Welsh, so only a few could understand. Wrexham, more or less, is in England, and only a few speak Welsh. Dafydd just walked up behind Gareth and said. "Ready to leave, sergeant," in his most assertive voice.

"Sir," came back the immediate response,

They both walked out of the door and around the corner to the car. "Thank god you are OK, I thought you were a gonna for a while, how do you feel?" enquired Dafydd.

"Bloody awful to be honest, there is no way I could stay there when a couple of paracetamols would do the trick."

As soon as Martin saw them, he leaped from the car, opened the rear door, "Get him in the back and get him comfortable. I will do the first leg of the journey, or do you want us to take you back to Dafydd's mum's?"

"Neither of you can manage without me, just drive, I will have something to eat and drink," he said, eyeing up all the food on the back seat, and with that, Martin drove out of the hospital and onto the A483 heading South. Apart from a bit of heavy traffic around Shrewsbury, they pulled up at the Telford services an hour later for a toilet break. After fiddling on his phone for the internet, he discovered the timing from Telford to Toddington and Cambridge to Toddington was about the same. He rang Chloe and told her to set off immediately, and they should meet up in just over an hour's time.

It wasn't until just after 4 o'clock that they pulled into Toddington Services, all three looking around for Chloe, it was Gareth who saw her first, standing by her car looking very cold, she didn't recognise them till Martin got out of the car, as soon as she saw him she ran over and threw her arms around him, she opened the boot of her car and removed a bag, locked her car, they put her in the front passenger seat as she knew the way around London.

Dafydd now took over the driving with Martin and Gareth in the back. They were quickly on their way. Chloe opened her bag and handed more sandwiches and flasks with all sorts of goodies to eat to Gareth's delight.

"I have come to the conclusion that women are the born providers of this world," said Gareth.

"And I am of the opinion that men, especially soldiers, are born eating machines. I have to say, Gareth, you are the best-looking dead man I have ever seen. How are you? The way Martin described you, I didn't think I would be seeing you again."

"Thank you for your concern, Chloe, but as you can see, they can't do anything without me, and even to the extent of dragging me out of bed. Personally, I think they prefer to drive my car." With that, they all laughed, relieving any tension.

They rejoined the motorway and continued down the M1. The traffic got heavier, much heavier, "Wrong time of day." Gareth said, stating the obvious. "Should we pull in somewhere and let these poor demented souls get home, as I am dying for a pee," and shortly after, pulled up at the London gateway services.

They all went to relieve themselves two at a time, noticing Gareth was now quite sprightly, they finished their coffees and sandwiches, filled the car up again, discussed where the heck everybody was going and how many people there were, and returned on the motorway at just after 6 o'clock, commenting that the traffic was no less heavy. It was at 7:30 when Gareth said as he negotiated all the traffic. "Have you noticed every other vehicle is an SUV, we are the only ones with real mud on, and use the thing for its correct use."

Shortly after, they turned left onto Great Russell Street, then around to the rear entrance on Montague Place, pulling up at the rear gates of the British Museum.

Chapter Twenty-Five

Chloe got out of the car and spoke into the intercom, returning as the gates opened electrically by a man pushing a button, who was also checking if it was indeed Professor Stone, not that he knew her.

They drove into a covered way, which then went into a cavernous room with wooden crates everywhere. Dafydd cut the engine, and it was so quiet that all you could hear was the engine ticking with the heat as it started to cool down. They all got out of the vehicle at the same time as two guards approached them. "Have you all got identification, please?" said one of the men with a clipboard. They all dived into their jacket pockets and produced differing IDs, which the guard wrote down on his pad, then he disappeared up a short flight of steps, returning a short while later with a small hand-held device. "I need to scan the box you have for any concealed weapons?"

They looked at Chloe for conformation as Dafydd removed the box from the back of the vehicle which was standing on the floor between his legs, she thought about the radio waves, "I think it would be OK but could you ring Doctor Spillner first, she is here and is expecting us, as these documents are over 1200 years old, I would prefer her to commit her reputation rather than mine for scanning anything in this box."

The guard retraced his tracks up the steps, and after a few moments, he came back down. "We will escort you into the laboratories where there are a number of people waiting for your arrival."

Dafydd adjusted the box back onto his back as he hauled it into position, and they all followed the two guards, first going down a large set of stone stairs and continuing along long corridors. "It's as bad as the bloody hospital," said Gareth.

They eventually walked into an expansive, well-lit room where there were benches, monitors, computers, and clever specialist machinery everywhere. They were warmly greeted by four people. Doctor Anne Spillner held her hand out to Chloe, and it was evident that they knew each other well. "We went to university together," she said as an explanation.

Doctor Spillner turned to her colleagues to introduce them, "Doctor Rarj Masoom, Doctor Alan Richards, and Doctor Jane Isaccs." We are all very excited about what you have for us."

While the Welshman removed the box from his back and placed it on the stainless-steel top Chloe introduced her group, placing her hand on Dafydd's shoulder and introduced him. "Dafydd Griffiths and Gareth Evans, both SAS officers who have managed to transport these articles from an exceptionally difficult place, this is Martin Ambrose who found out by complete accident he was related to the well-known, none mythical person named Merlin, he has kindly donated what is possibly the best preserved piece of social history this country has ever known, no matter how disturbing we may find what is written in the years ahead of us."

One of the doctor curators was about to undo the Velcro straps when Martin stepped forward and said, "I am still uncomfortable about this tome being here, so if you don't mind, I will remove it for you." He undid all the Velcro straps, then carefully and reverently, with some difficulty with the weight, he removed the ancient documents from the box and placed them on the work surface. The Leather top, still in place that had protected these ancient documents for over 1200 years, now looked far older than it did when it was back in the cave. Once the book was laid there he turned the 8th century cover that had protected it for all those years and placed it at its side, he then turned to the page with the date, and turned to another page containing the now familiar writings, he stood back for them to gaze in wonder at the ancient script which could reveal so much to these learned people, whether they could decipher it that quick he had no way of knowing. The four academics all stared while the team that had brought it watched on.

Doctor Masoom, who was the head of the department, said. "We really need to preserve these manuscripts, we will put them into an air tight glass container, then academics can see and inspect them before we decide how best they can be preserved, he reached over to close the book when total disaster struck, the minute his hands touched the manuscript, the entire book started to crumble, in seconds all that was left was a pile of grey dust.

They all stared in unbelievable wonder at what had just happened in front of their very eyes. They turned and looked at the Asian gentleman Doctor, who unwittingly had destroyed something beyond measure or price. The look of astonished disbelief and fear was as if he was about to make a run for cover as the man-made mountain named Gareth moved towards him. It was Martin who broke the silence as he raised his arm with his hand outstretched, and said in that calming voice.

"I thought something like this would happen; to be honest, I thought it would have happened sooner than it has. Merlin was what today would be called or termed as a wizard; he probably only referred to himself as scholarly." Then, after witnessing the disbelieving last few moments, this calm voice was excusing the destruction of his family's and that of the nation's heritage, added, "A month or so ago, Merlin was nothing but a myth, a legend, based on a cleaver story by Geoffrey of Monmouth, in which for hundreds of years have entertained us, along with the fabled Arthurian folklore addition. Now whether we admit that he was, or wasn't some type of wizard, he almost certainly bewitched this book some way to self-destroy if anybody outside his family, or maybe anybody of none Welsh birth touched it, but with all due respects someone from a totally different culture would have been completely alien to him, it could have happened to anybody from abroad or with a foreign DNA.

The Welsh, which is what these two gentlemen are, are some of the original and ancient Britons, and almost certainly is what Merlin was. I suppose I must belong to that category of people, along with Chloe, as we have handled the book quite extensively. I was right all along when I said to Chloe that it should remain in the cave where I found it. In fact, since we have discovered it, one man has been killed, both Gareth and I have been beaten up and taken to the hospital, both Chloe's and my houses have been broken into, and the police have their hands full now trying to apprehend three dangerous men, and what for? Some old bits of paper, and what was written on them." Martin shook his head, not knowing what else to add, turned and walked out of the door, followed by Dafydd and Gareth, and then, hesitantly, Chloe, bringing up the rear, signalling to her friend that she would ring her later.

They retraced their steps along the corridors and into the area where their Nissan was parked, looking filthy due to the bright lights and white walls, Dafydd said to the two guards. "Can you open the doors? We are all off home.

As soon as they were on their way, Gareth was behind the steering wheel while Dafydd put in the Welsh address on the Satnav, then asked. "Chloe, do you want to go and pick up your car from the services or go straight back to Wales?"

Chapter Twenty-Six

While Martin and his fellow passengers were on their way out of London, the murder hunt had been stepped up, more police officers had been drafted in, both from North Wales, Mercia, and Cambridge, the acting senior officer being Detective Inspector Brown. Stanley Gibson had been re-arrested and brought in to be interrogated by Detective Collins, who was an expert interviewer and would relate anything that would help the case to DI. Brown. Ironically, Gibson was still refusing to believe he had done anything wrong. "OK. First, you get papers you told our local bobby that you got off the internet, is that correct?"

"Yes, but…."

"Next, you sent a private investigator to find an address in North Wales?"

"Yes, but only so I could….."

"Next, you go to that address and break into his house, cut open a briefcase, and steal some papers?"

"Yes, only so I could….."

"Next, you realise you are useless at being discreet, which I can agree with, so you go and get some help?"

There was silence as the penny was dropping in Gibson's mind, and he knew the people he had hired had killed someone, so he changed his answer. "No comment."

"Those people may be responsible for murder and GBH. You will be held accountable for your part of that. Do you still not want a brief?"

"Yes." The inspector scooped up all the paperwork and went out of the interview room. They locked Gibson down in the cells to gather further evidence.

DI Brown and DS Allsop arrived back in Corwen police station at 6 o'clock, to see how things were progressing, only to find that a few moments previously, two local bobbies had been called out to attend a road traffic collision involving two vehicles, one had been flagged up as a wanted car, and had been stolen in Cambridge, the constable knowing that this wasn't the first incident regarding that town, thought it might have a bearing on something more sinister and had called into Corwen to report. "We are just outside the village of Pen-y-stryt; all services are now in attendance," said one of the constables, and continued. "A family which included a tiny baby were travelling in one direction have all been pronounced dead at the scene, the driver of the wanted vehicle is also dead, but this is the strange bit, we found another man halfway across a field, the only reason we found him he was calling out in agony, he had collapsed with multiple internal injuries, according to a paramedic, who have only just seen him, said he don't think he will live but are getting him ready to take to hospital. Now the boot of the stolen car was open, indicating that we think items have been removed, but as there was nothing on the man halfway across the field, we think a third man may now be on the run. I hope that's some help to you."

They had the maps out on desks, discussing where their third man could have got to; at least, all roadblocks could be eased. It wasn't for another hour that a report came in that a car had been reported stolen from outside a pub, not that far from where the RTC had occurred. "That's no coincidence," said Brown. "Can we get an APB (All-Points Bulletin) out as soon as possible?"

"Already done, and that's all we can do for the time being. Would you like some fish and chips? One of the officers is going across the road to get some," said one of the Welsh policemen. Brown opened his wallet and took a £20 note out and handed it to him, telling him that it would go towards the bill.

"OK," said Brown, going back to the maps. "Which way would he go to get onto the M6 from there?" he said, pointing to the name of the little village in which there was no way he was going to even try to pronounce it.

"He'll go around Wrexham along the A534 to Nantwich, then take the A500 till he hits the M6," said an officer without even looking at the map. "I've done it hundreds of times."

"How long will that take?"

"This time of night, about an hour, possibly a bit more, he will probably rest up at Keele services. Anybody who has been in a serious accident would need to rest, and that is only another 20 minutes away."

"Right, get Stoke on Trent boys on the line and see if they would do a quick recce at Keele, to see if they can see the stolen car, warn them he could be armed though."

While they were waiting for any response, Brown's mobile rang, he answered it, and was surprised to hear Martin. "Inspector, this is Martin Ambrose here. We have just left the British Museum and are on our way back. We managed to get the book into the museum without too much trouble, unfortunately, it turned to dust, so the whole exercise has been a complete waste of time, I am afraid."

"Mr. Ambrose, it may have been a complete waste of your time, but the police don't measure success or failure in that way, we have several more deaths to get to the bottom of, a potential serious theft of national treasure, and if it wasn't for the greed, of whoever started out to obtain those parchments in the first place, many people would still be alive. However, I can tell the North Wales police to stand down, which I think they may well have done anyway. Thank you for ringing me. I am sorry it never worked out the way you had intended. Bye for now."

The man in the stolen Volvo car had just woken up, realising he ached all over, his mouth felt like the bottom of a parrot's cage, not that he had ever eaten anything from the bottom of a parrot's cage. He desperately needed to go to the toilet and get a coffee. He virtually fell out of the car and limped across the forecourt in the pouring rain; he hadn't the energy to carry the heavy box into the cafe.

Even though he had had a good hours' sleep and was feeling slightly more refreshed, he still felt very ill. It was nearly 30 minutes later, returning through the foyer after eating a full English breakfast, along with two coffees, when he noticed blue flashing lights. It didn't take him long to realise police were surrounding the Volvo. He quickly ducked back into the cafe, then thought they had no idea who they were looking for, but it wouldn't take them long to find out. At least it would give him some time to get away. Trying to ignore the pains he still had in his legs; he walked as steady as he could to where the lorries were parked.

Nowadays, it's not as easy to get a lift from lorry drivers as it used to be. It was the third one who told him he could take him as far as Leicester. He jumped in, well, crawled in would be a better description. Just as the lorry started pulling out a police car pulled in front of him, mystified by this sudden hold-up the lorry driver stuck his head out of his window to enquire what the problem was, by this time another policeman had opened the passenger door and removed his fugitive, cuffed him and unceremoniously pushed him into the back of a police car, the first policeman then asked. "When did you pick up your passenger, sir?"

"Just now, I often do. The company breaks up the tedious journey somewhat."

"Does your company know you give lifts?"

"I own the lorry, so that doesn't apply to me."

Sergeant Clarke rang Corwen station to tell them they had apprehended their man. "We are now waiting for a low loader to pick up the stolen car," they also told Brown. "It will go back to Stoke-on-Trent station lock-up and wait there until further instructions."

"That would be great. Make sure our man is locked up. I will get somebody to pick him up tomorrow. I will also organise the transfer of the Volvo, but I don't know when that will be. By the way, what was in the box?"

"We have removed it from the vehicle and at the moment it's in the boot of my car, I will not open it, that would involve more paperwork, we just haven't the resources at the moment, we are in the middle of a manhunt for a child abductor, our men just happened to be here, I will leave it for you to collect at the same time as your man, it was nice that we were able to help you."

"Well, I'm very grateful," said Brown, and thanked him for his prompt and efficient actions. After the two detectives and the other officers had finished their fish and chip supper, they shook hands all round, then left the Corwen police station and drove back to Cambridge.

On the way back, DS Allsop said, "Do you know I

never realised just how beautiful Wales was, also the Welsh up here don't talk like the lot down in South Wales, in fact I could move here quite easily, do they want English police, do you think?"

"I haven't a clue, sergeant, but you would have to learn Welsh first, correction, have to learn to speak English first, then go on to Welsh. I think you would be better just taking your holidays here."

Chapter Twenty-Seven

Following a phone call, DI Brown went back to see Martin Ambrose a few days later in North Wales. It was just after 10 o'clock when he pulled up outside the neat farmhouse and knocked on the kitchen door. This time, he had brought the new detective sergeant Shirley Draycott with him. "Morning, Mr. Ambrose, you look a lot better since the last time I saw you."

"For a reply, he opened the door wider. "Coffee?" and ushered the two in.

Once they were all seated, Shirley removed her notebook to start taking notes. "Can you repeat for me the exact chain of events that happened before, during, and after the visit to the British Museum?"

"I can do better than that, both Chloe and I have typed the entire episode down for you, and we did it separately, and we signed them for you," and handed over the sheets of paper, followed by two coffees.

"That's marvellous, thank you. It will save me some time, but I still have to ask, that book, was it written by Merlin then?"

"Oh yes, but there is now no proof, of course. We

have all the notes, but they amount to nothing other than hearsay. Tell us what happened to the other box and the men. I take it you caught them?"

Reluctantly, Brown reiterated the events leading up to the arrest of the man with the box, who claims he never shot anybody. The death of both the family and the driver of the getaway car, and the third man is extremely badly injured and not expected to live. Also, we have arrested and charged Mr. Stanley Gibson, who, by the way, still denies any involvement. But we have more than enough to charge him for all manner of offences. We will continue to gather evidence from two other police forces. The car the villains stole, as well as the car they used as a getaway, are both with forensics. Oh, there is one bit of good news…. some of the artefacts you used to pad out the decoy box have been given to our local museum. They are quite excited about them, but I have no idea what they are. Well, I am now going to the Griffiths to get some more statements." So after shaking hands all around, the two police inspectors drove off.

After Inspector Brown had left, Martin said to Chloe. "Let's go up to Merlin's cave and have one more look round." Now, in a much cheerier mood than he had felt for a long time. "At least we can say goodbye to Merlin as much as anything. I doubt if we will be going up there so often now. I think, under the circumstances, I will leave his remains exactly where they are and completely undisturbed."

They donned their warmest clothes. It was still bitterly cold. Martin jumped onto the new quad, and Chloe slid in behind. They pulled out of the barn and headed towards the cave. It still took the best part of an hour before Martin laid his hand on the rock to the entrance. It opened as it always did, and with very little sound.

They turned on their torches as they went in. It felt empty without the oversized book resting on the side where it had lain for so many years, and had probably been penned there, or at least some of it was.

Martin then walked into the bedchamber and looked kindly at his old ancestor, well, what was left of him. He had no idea why he said it, but he apologised anyway for removing his life's work from the cave. He thanked him for trying to pass on the correct long-lost information, and underestimated his power and his wisdom to protect that information, even after all these years, from anybody other than a family member or one with Celtic blood. He turned back towards the entrance only to see Chloe silhouetted in the doorway. She held the lantern at such an angle that he could see her long hair hanging down with a woollen hat on top. She was staring at him with her mouth open. "Sorry, I was just saying my goodbyes."

She stared at him and slowly shook her head. It was then, after seeing her standing in that doorway, looking at her beautiful, rounded face from the light she was holding. Martin looked just above her head; in a niche set into a stone above the doorway, was something giving off reflective light. He reached up and took down two metal objects. One looked like a beaker, the other a plate. He gestured for Chloe to go back outside. Once there, they examined the articles. "Do you think they are gold?" he asked her.

She was still staring at him, then said, ignoring the articles he was holding, "Did you know you were speaking in that mixture of Latin and Old English, like the language throughout Merlin's book? I could only understand a bit of what you were saying, but it sounded really strange."

"I was doing what? Am I still talking like that now?"

"No, that really is very weird," she said, still shaking her head. "Let's have a look at what you have," she said, taking the beaker into her own hands. "Looks very much like gold," she said as she examined the beaker more closely. "They are beautiful. What are you going to do with them?"

"A very good question," he looked for inspiration in Chloe's face, then turned round and replaced them exactly as he had found them. "I think we have removed enough of Merlin's belongings as it is. Let's go home and leave Merlin in peace."

When they returned with bright red cheeks, they prepared lunch of BLTs, as they had decided to go out to the grouse for dinner later, then Martin said. "By the way, I haven't told you that I went back to the house where I was born and brought up. I think I told you it was in Rutland. I always thought it belonged to the Duke of Rutland's estate. I was wrong; I own it along with 25 acres. It's looking decidedly in need of some serious TLC. Anyway, I searched throughout the property for some clues that might reveal themselves to indicate I was related to Merlin."

"And did you find anything?" she asked, putting all the ingredients together for their meal and putting the sandwiches onto plates to eat in the lounge.

For an answer, Martin disappeared from the room, returning a few moments later. "I found this box, it was inside another which was buried under some quarry tiles which were situated under the stairs," he produced the little, very ornate, heavily embossed, solid gold box which he had removed from the bank, now that all the danger had passed.

Chloe picked up the little box and studied it. "This is absolutely exquisite," she turned it over in her hands. "How old is it?"

"Not sure, not as old as Merlin, that's for certain. The hallmarks are on the base. But I don't know how to read them. Let's finish our sandwiches first."

As soon as Chloe had eaten and wiped her mouth with a napkin, she asked in an excited voice. "Got a magnifying glass."

Martin produced a glass, pencil, and paper, then picked up the box and read out the assay marks.

"The first is TM&Co, the next is 22, the third symbol is a shield with three things on it, which look like sheaves of wheat, next a letter 'U', and the last is some sort of head, what does all that represent?"

For an answer, Chloe took out her laptop. "There's an app called assay wizard," she tapped a few keys, and looked down at what she had just written down on the pad. "According to this, it was manufactured in Chester. The TM&Co means it was assayed for a certain Thomas Marshal. The 22 signifies it is 22-carat gold. What is the font of the U?"

"Like a Roman numeral."

Manufactured in 1838, and the head could be a leopard, so there you are,1838. To me, it looks like it was made yesterday. Are you sure it hasn't still got its bar code on?" and laughed. "Anyway, you can take it to a jeweller. They will tell you immediately."

"You must be joking," he then produced a small gold coloured 30 mm long cylindrical piece with a small intricately carved handle and handed it to Chloe. "Try using this key," he said, indicating the tiny round hole just below the top of the box.

Taking the key, she slipped it into the hole. Nothing happened. She turned it, but still nothing happened. She pushed it, and the top clicked open. The only thing inside was a small piece of parchment with very small writing on it. It was the same script written on all those other pages. She looked enquiringly at Martin. "Can you read this?"

"Ironically, yes, I can, as if it were English."

"I can make out some of the words just as before. What does it say? Is it important or even indicative of anything written in the book?"

"It's extremely pertinent to Merlin. That bit of parchment was probably written by Merlin himself in his last years of life. However old he was at the time, I'm not sure, but that has been passed down through my family. How he passed it on from that cave, I am again unsure. The box is not that old. Well, we have just dated it; one of my ancestors thought that parchment worthy of that magnificent box."

"Well, for goodness's sake, Martin, you can be annoying at times. What does it say on the note?"

"It's more of what it doesn't say. If you were able to read it out, it sounds better than the way it's written down. It tells me about a hidden cave that can only be opened by a member of the Ambrosins family. But it doesn't tell me where the cave is.

He says he has written down everything that he has done or has happened and hopes it will be of use in years henceforth.

By the way, it's not written in this way. He writes in a way that very few people could read, but you know that. Merlin calls the language he writes as Vrondil. It's what people spoke but never wrote down. You were spot on about the transition period, where the indigenous people of Britain were forced out by the Romans, as well as all the other tribes at that time. The language forced on them was too difficult to use by these natives, so it was very mixed up. Hence, the reason you had so much trouble translating it.

However, Vrondil was used extensively for the best part of 300 years. Do you want to spend Christmas here and," err, he hesitated for a moment before blurting out, "Shall we get married?"

About the Author

The author started his working life as a plumber way back in 1963. After some 40 years, including many different aspects of the plumbing world, he finished his career after a further 10 years as a lecturer in plumbing at both Worcester and Hereford Colleges of Technology. He has three children and five grandchildren. Robin started writing a historical novel over 35 years ago and has written five more stand-alone novels since. After completing *'From Rags with Brains'* his first published work, this new novel, *'Merlin's Return'* becomes his second published book. He now lives with his wife in Shropshire and is still writing.